Ballyferme

l

C000131647

Home Boys Home

Yet Another Collection Of Creative Writing In The Nuclear War On Homelessness

Ballyer Press

ISBN-13:
9798448437182

All Profits from this book will be donated to
The Simon Community

Limited Edition

/160

Simon

By Ballyer Press.

Homelessness is a Frankenstein pus-pimple on the scaldy face of Irish society that keeps getting more ginormous and scabby with each passing day the government fails to build any houses. So this is yet another collection of creative writing by a bunch of naive writers in the nuclear war on homelessness.

A poem, a story or an essay won't change the world so don't hold your breath that this will do anything to mitigate homelessness in any way. However, what it can do, fingers and heart crossed, is raise a little money for the Simon Community as all proceeds from this book will be dropped from a height into their helping hands.

Caveat: Not all writing in this collection is on the subject of homelessness. It also contains nuts, sugar, gluten, fat, earth, wind and fire too.

Buy this book and feel young, gifted and righteous.

Cover it with flowery wallpaper to keep it pristine and smelling of tulips forever.

Contents

Dedicated to Nicky Earley

Introduction:

21st century Ireland has been plagued by crisis. From the banking crash of 2008 to Covid-19, crises have rocked society to the core.

But the deepest crisis of the 21st Century is that of housing and homelessness. It's a crisis that has its origins in the political decisions of the 1990's and early 2000's when successive governments decided to fuel a speculative housing boom. At the same time the provision of social housing was undermined, stigmatised and de-prioritised with virtually no social housing being built for at least a decade.

With Fine Gael in government since 2011 what was already a crisis has become an emergency. The reliance on the private market to supply housing has utterly failed. Fine Gael's empty promises to sort out the housing crisis through their Rebuilding Ireland plan gave a leg up to private developers and landlords through HAP schemes and the sell-off of public land to private developers for a small percentage of social housing. International investment funds (known as vulture funds) were invited in by Fine Gael's Michael Noonan and have wreaked havoc on the housing market by pushing prices and rents up.

This approach has completely failed the hundreds of thousands of people who are in need of housing. It has created a staggering increase in rents and pushed house prices way beyond affordability for most. Those with the most need have been the hardest hit. The lack of social housing has pushed low income families in to homelessness.

Families with disabilities, from the Travelling community, migrants and lone parents have been disproportionately affected. Homeless numbers were steadily increasing with over 10 000 people in emergency accommodation at its height. We now have a generation of young people who will be privately renting all their lives at extraordinary costs.

The Fianna Fail, Fine Gael and Green Party coalition published their Housing For All document in September 2021. The document contains some impressive numbers and promises about increased social housing and new affordable housing schemes. But if you read the small print it becomes clear that this is just more of the same. It represents a continued reliance on the private market to provide housing with some subsidies for private developers.

Instead of these failed policies we need real radical action on housing. We need to guarantee the right to housing in the constitution. We need to create public housing available to everyone regardless of their income. We should follow best practice in European countries such as Austria and Sweden through which we can create sustainable mixed communities. We need a Housing First approach linked to services for those with multiple needs. We need to tackle the shortage of building workers by creating more apprenticeships and a public construction company offering long term contracts and decent pay and conditions for workers.

To do all this, we need a change of government. But we need much more than that. We need a movement of people power and workers to challenge the current economic system and put homes for people before the profits of developers.

Madeleine Johansson
People Before Profit
Councillor on South Dublin County Council

Plovdiv Live Test
by
Rob Doyle

The following text was written 'live' in front of an audience at Sklad Tobacco City in Plovdiv, Bulgaria, on 23 April 2019, as part of an interdisciplinary performance which also involved the writers Christos Ikonomou, Edy Poppy, Vladimir Martinovski and Ivan Dimitrov, the musician Rossen Zahariev, and the artist Dimitar Shopov. Before the performance commenced, audience members were asked to write words on pieces of paper. I was then given the collected words. With a laptop connected to a projector, I wrote a text that included as many of the words as I could use (Ivan Dimitrov wrote a separate text projected alongside mine, using words submitted in the Bulgarian language). A video of the performance can be seen at https://youtu.be/hGRB-H3dWGM

She met him at a drum and bass night in a club under a disused railway station at the edge of the city. They got high and talked about masculinity, courage, despair. In an alley a prostitute sang; I think it was a protest song but I can't be sure. 'Democracy?', said the lissom girl, her eyes wide and sparkling. 'Don't make me laugh.'

Desire diffused across the dimensions of the night. Anything seemed possible (at least, that's how it felt to her). She wondered whether he had an erection, but she couldn't be certain. Later they broke into a deserted factory, some crumbling relic of disintegrated Socialism.

On the walls there was hallucinatory graffiti, like the nightmares of a psychotic: ABOLISH LIBERTY! Bizarre imagery like scenes from Hell.

'Is this hell?' he asks. He seems innocent when he says it, not afraid. She loved him then.

'Loneliness and amusement are close to one another,' she said.
'So are gardens and sleep', he said. Then he laughed.

Did she have a name? Did he? I know they did, but when the dream was over I had forgotten them.

*

At a karaoke bar in a sprawling Japanese city (Osaka? Tokyo? Kyoto?) a man with one eye and a soft beautiful voice sings the saddest song anyone ever heard. There is no audience - he sings to an empty room. The music fades, the man himself is gone.
*

The woman in the crumbling house near the motorway is reading a book called *Responsibility*. Her husband is dead. His body is decaying in the small upstairs room at the back of the house.

('How long has he been there?' 'How should I know?' The teenagers soon get bored and wander off to throw stones at the windows of abandoned factories.)

She starts drinking port each morning at eleven o'clock. On Tuesdays and Thursdays she waits till noon. I imagine she's happy, though that's not what the others say.

Loneliness, despair - these are experiences for the young, she thinks. Good to be done with all that: she believes herself to be free, and who am I to argue.

'Sleep is the cousin of death', her husband used to say. It had always annoyed her. And now look at him. In the afternoons she wanders out beyond the motorway: dusty industrial wasteland, a shattered poetry. Maybe I'll find a pet, she thinks, then she laughs. Those drug-addled teenagers used to take photographs out here with antique cameras, she recalls, and have those parties where they got up to who knows what. You couldn't tell girls from boys any more. Everything was melting together. She was tired of the world and its demands.

One night she takes the train into the city. She watches a show in a theatre that is all but empty; a few scattered perverts, winos, junkies, couples looking for careless kicks. The show is incomprehensible: she's not even sure which language they're speaking (if indeed it is a language).

A woman walks out onto the stage, bathed in blue light. She begins to sing, with no instruments playing, only a voice, a strange song with a melody that reminds her of certain anguished faces from decades ago. Halfway through the song, the singer falters, her voice breaks down: she is weeping softly. Now a man appears on the stage. He is wearing a navy suit, his eyes look Satanic. He peers at each member of the audience in turn. When he looks at the woman, he pauses for a moment, and then he says: 'This piece has now concluded.'

Handout
by
John Healy

The light which comes slowly and coldly to a shop doorway in winter woke the man who began coughing his guts up as he reached out to feel for his bag as if that was the most he had to lose. He took a stale crust from the bag and began trying his teeth out on it afterwards when he had finished his breakfast he continued sitting amongst the crumbs. A smell had begun to arise from his frail body stripped of flesh by hunger and human resentment, it was not possible in the congested doorway to avoid the smell of piss. But how can a man sleep in this condition when he knows what he faces when he awakes how can he slumber on the edge of a doorway? Where does his peace come from?

Outside the post office the Christmas choir were singing of redemption. A lot of it surprised him for since he had been living on the street it had never occurred to him that Christmas could be taken seriously.

As he began contemplating his future investing the most unpromising situations with hope it started to rain, which turned to sleet but the man continued to sit in the dripping doorway whatever might happen next could not be worse because homelessness had been imposed by man.

His little dog had died from the cold some time ago then his mate who had occupied the space opposite him had died, he had watched his heels jerk as they dragged his body away. All afternoon the man continued to sit there, now and then he held out his hand it was more of a mechanical gesture to beg passers-by too involved in the joy of Christmas to stop. Though those that were kind dropped a few coins as they passed into his hand those who were less kind hurried past refusing to see what could only upset them.

But he was to lonely to care and to bitter for home and he sat in the doorway with his memories and his hand held out. He was once a married man with children a house and a job but cuts had cost him his job then his house and finally his wife and children now the cord that had bound him to life was broken. When government policy alters the meaning of life this is what is arrived at.

The carol singers were still in full voice singing of how Christ's coming would bring happiness to each and everyone but the man knew different.

In the absence of rejoicing he continued to sit with his hand held out.

As the night turned into morning once more, he was still sitting there in his cardboard house with his hand out and his eyes wide open staring into the white dawn but he saw nothing out of those eyes he had frozen into that position during the night. When the early morning street cleaner came by he stopped to gaze at the man but had no means of removing the body.

It seems the government had overlooked what to do about the dead in revising its homelessness policy?

Article on Homelessness
by
Frankie Gaffney

teach, g. tighe, d. tigh, pl. tighthe and tighe, m. (in M. tigh, pron. tig genly. is the usual nom. form; teach in poetry in nom. and dat.; in Con. and Don. teach is nom. and dat.), a house, a mansion; teach te teolaidhe, a warm, comfortable house; isteach, in (after verbs of motion); istigh, inside (of rest); teach oibridhe, a labourer's cottage.

—*Foclóir Gaedhilge agus Béarlaan*, by Rev. Patrick S. Dinneen, M.A.

gaff /gaef/ (colloq.), a house or home (origin obscure; cf. Beale: 'the most common prison word for a dwelling-place, house, or room'*).* 'Are yiz coming back to my gaff?'

—*A Dictionary of Hiberno-English*, by Terence Patrick Dolan

The disparity between Hiberno-English and Irish words for *house* shown above is perhaps less than accidental. There is a certain serendipity to how they reflect distinct cultural circumstances that arose in the change from a Gaelic proto-feudal society, in which each person was still inextricably enmeshed in their tribe, to today's Anglicised hyper-capitalist state, with its increasing social isolation. We should not be under any illusion that because our technology is more advanced, today's society is necessarily superior. Although social provision has been professionalised, it has also been pared down. If its administration is more efficient, there is a lot wanting in the detail—and there, of course, is where the devil lies.

In a document known as "Bee-Judgements", cravings during pregnancy were recognised and provided for by the Gaelic law tracts, which obliged the "owner of a bee-swarm to supply his neighbours with honey gratis should any of their wives require it" (Ó Cróinín, p. 132).

While the Anglicised state founded in 1922 never made good on the promise of the *Proclamation* to "cherish all the children of the nation equally", Gaelic society made provisions like these from conception on, placing obligations on wider society to assist others. Power and status came with responsibilities and obligations. Today, the opposite is the case—one of the benefits of power and wealth today is the ability to shirk duty entirely. The wealthiest in our society can evade taxes, have the means to avoid scrutiny by the police, can escape the consequences of almost any action through the legal system, and receive bailouts to subsidise any major losses. In Gaelic Ireland the tribe gathered for kingship inauguration feasts, in which the whole community was provided with meat in symbolic communion with their incumbent king.

Today's potlatches funnel wealth from the poor to the rich to pay for their gambling mistakes caused by the vicissitudes of a turbulent stock market. The sociality of Gaelic Ireland was not socialism, but it was much more socially minded than the country in which we live today.

This not to paint some picture of pre-invasion Ireland as some Arcadian idyll. It wasn't. Aside from being patriarchal, and often brutally violent, Gaelic Ireland was moving towards feudalism before the Anglo-Norman invasion, following a European wide trend. This island would likely have ended up a capitalist state whether or not the English invaded. And what is often ignored is the fact that its beginnings were no less problematic than its ends. We don't know what language the people who built Newgrange spoke—but it wasn't Irish.

The Celts most likely arrived on this island the same way the Anglo-Normans did—on horses, carrying swords, and ready to forcibly assimilate or simply dispossess the native culture. This is an important point—those who whip up animus and fear around different ethnicities should be made face the contrast with how our ancestors—Celts, Vikings, Normans, and English—arrived here, and how immigrants now arrive. The Celts brought with them the domesticated horse, and introduced an Indo-European language to the island, a language family that has been prevalent everywhere from Galway, to London, to Paris, to Vladivostok, to Geneva, to Mumbai. We are part of this broader expansionist culture of conquest, although that is often forgotten.

We don't know much about the cultures that the Indo-European peoples replaced, but given the shape and symbolism of the passage tombs they built in Ireland, it is possible they were matriarchal, and they obviously had the high level of organisation necessary to carry out such monumental works of public architecture. So far as we know, their society was obliterated, by the very culture from which we not only proudly claim ancestry, but mourn the oppression and conquest of.

In a further irony, however, many of those who rightly decry the injustices perpetrated against Irish people and the loss of our language and culture because of English colonialism are now keen to assist in the project of U.S. imperialism—enthusiastically and uncritically importing dumbed-down American politics and culture that have little or no relevance or applicability to Ireland, and are typically inane and incoherent even in America, where they emanate from bourgeois universities like the farts of a dyspeptic old professor who's had too much foie gras and Beaujolais. Local dialect has been replaced with a Kardashiaccent, dialectics replaced by dogma, materialism by mantra.

Free-market fundamentalist Margaret Thatcher famously asserted "there is no such thing as society". While ridiculed for this statement, it is an accurate description of the world she wanted to create—in which competition not co-operation would define human relations. Lesser known is the subsequent sentence: "There are individual men and women and there are families." In reality, we are moving swiftly away from even this level of social structure, with the reduced modern conception of the family (as a nuclear unit of parents and their offspring) as an economic unit, towards the total atomisation of individual men and women alone, existing as solitary individuals, in theory free to choose their relationships at their pleasure, in practice devoid of the opportunity to form and maintain permanent healthy relationships of any sort. In Ireland the trend can be clearly seen as we transitioned from tribalism, to feudalism, to capitalism, and now to late-capitalism, in the obliteration of the secure type of homes needed to form a family. There has been an increasing atomisation of society in tandem with the concentration of wealth.

The basic unit in Gaelic Ireland was not the individual, or even the family (in Thatcher's sense of the word), but the extended family, or *derbfine* (true kin). To make good on the project of the Proclamation, we need to extend the concept of the tribe to embrace everyone who lives on this island, apply to them the Gaelic idea of derbfine, and make sure they have equal opportunities to provide for themselves in the manner which the enormous technological advances since Gaelic times allow us to. This means reverting to more communal forms of ownership, not only in clichéd Marxist terms of the means of production, but also in terms of the land and buildings in which people actually live.

Current forms of land ownership are an English importation, and in terms of the broad scope of human history have existed for only the blink of an eye. Communal forms of land ownership have a much longer tradition on this island, having existed uncorrupted on this island for thousands of years. Land held in common creates a much more stable society, one that is not buffeted by impersonal forces of the market. This form of living comes more naturally to us than the very belated capitalist forms, which alienate us from each other, and commercialise relationships which should be natural and voluntary.

There is no Hiberno-English word for tent. But the Irish word is *puball*, which comes from the Latin papilio, which also meant butterfly. Some sources claim that this etymology derives from a resemblance between a butterfly's wings and the fabric of a tent—but I wonder if tents back then, generally used for military purposes, were so brightly patinated. If I were to guess, I suspect a butterfly's impermanence has something to do with the derivation of the word. In Dublin in 2020, tents litter the canals. These "homes" are a function of a system of private ownership and inheritance which inevitably, as a matter of course, dispossess most of its children. James Joyce famously declared Ireland to be "the sow that eats her farrow", but perhaps even that is too complimentary for what we have become. Less scholastic Dubliners have been known to look at the tents and say "I wouldn't put a pig in it". Let us do better.

The March Home
by
Kit De Waal

My father was a dreamer. He walked to work, clocked in, bent his back to the lathe and his dreams dissolved in the milky oil on the knurling bench, in the hot factory noise.

He took his sandwiches to the canal, watched the wind worry the skin of the water and dreamed of swaying in a crow's nest angled against the ocean, sea salt on his lips. At night, he churned his sheets, cutting swathes through savannah grass on sun-browned legs to camp fires and penny-whistle songs under indigo skies.

But always the rain came, screaming against the window and rivered over his dreams. Drowned them. So, he left us and learned to drink instead. He sang sour songs for coins in his hat, for stupoured days and black nights.

Then, one day he woke up in a yellow field with June birds shaping circles in a wide sky. He crumbed warm soil between his fingers and found three stones in his palm. One for each of us. And this time, when the rain came, it washed his pebbles bright - ruby, violet, green-veined opalescence. They clicked together in his pocket keeping time on his march home.

And his dreams became my bedtime stories, one stone on my pillow each night, a dragon's eye, a star, a pirate's treasure. And, on my wedding day, he sewed his stones into the hem of my dress. 'For your journey', he said.

Today, I squeezed his hand around them. They fell, grey and brown against the white sheet.

All Eyes On Me
by
Paul McVeigh

Rocco watched Miss walk around his table and stop, look at them one-by-one; backs straight, arms folded, fingers-on-lips for *shush*. She was deciding who got her first. On the wall behind, the behaviour chart showed everyone back to zero because it was Monday. Rocco loved Mondays. Black marks gone. Last week forgotten. Rocco's slate all fresh and so, so clean.

Miss chose, coming opposite Rocco, leaning over Tommy's head.

'Well done,' Miss smiled, 'you've really taken your time with this, haven't you?' She rested her hand on the boy's head. 'I'm sure you're going to grow up to be an artist.'

Tommy beamed the kind of smile Rocco practised for hours in front of the mirror but just couldn't get right.

Miss continued her circuit, her hand coming to rest on Jessica's shoulder. She kneeled down and whispered things causing blushes and giggles from the little girl. Rocco could imagine what she'd said.

A breeze came through the open window and blew a strand of hair loose across Miss's face. Rocco went straight over to Miss, and with his fingertips, super, super softly, tucked the strand behind her ear.

'Sit down, Rocco', Miss said, looking at the hand he'd touched her with.

Rocco looked at what her eyes could see; tiny cuts on his fingers and thick dirt under his nails. He hid his hands behind his back. Miss smiled the way she smiled only at Rocco, with her eyes nearly closed.

Rocco went back and sat on his seat, tucked his chair right in, tummy squashed tight into the table's edge and rested his arms on the large white sheet in front of him. He'd drawn their house, just like Miss had asked, but with a pretend garden, a pretend dog (he'd even written *woof! woof!* above the dog's head!) and a pretend bike leaning against the door. He had drawn his mammy with a pretend daddy.

It was Rocco's turn next but one and he couldn't wait to show Miss. He wanted to fix his dirty hands so he spat on them and rubbed on his trousers. He should have washed his hands before he went to bed last night, but there'd been a party and mum had let him sit up late. Auntie Kelly let him taste her wine and everyone laughed at him when he said it was disgusting. He made himself stay awake until everyone left so he could help mum upstairs. And so no-one would stay over. When he woke up this morning, he was already late for school so he didn't have time to wash. He'd have gotten a black mark for being late but there was no rule about being dirty. Not on the behaviour board anyway. When he found his uniform, unwashed, still in the washing machine where he'd put it on Friday, he sprayed it with the air-freshener from the toilet. Sprayed his hair too because Miss doesn't like the smell of Mammy's cigarettes.

Rocco stretched and yawned and his drawing came with him, stuck to the sweat on his forearms. He peeled the sheet off and saw dark stains on the fat of his arms and much, much worse, grey-black clouds of smudge on his page. He wouldn't get upset even though he'd worked so, so hard. Miss would see beneath the smudges, he was sure. They didn't change how good the work was underneath. He looked at the behaviour chart. His, the only name with a special column of its own.

'Lend me your rubber,' Rocco nudged Declan.

'No. Get your own'.

Miss stopped at Sam. 'What beautiful colours,' she said. 'I-am-list-en-ing,' she sang.

'I-am-list-en-ing,' everyone sang back, downed their pencils, folded their arms and looked at Miss. Everyone loved drawing class, especially on a hot afternoon, all on their best behaviour so Miss wouldn't make them do *real* school work.

'Look at this,' she said, holding up Sam's book. 'Isn't this wonderful? Why do I like this sooo much, Caterpillar Class?'

'Because of the colours.'

'Because it's so neat.'

Because it's Sam's, Rocco wanted to say. *Because you always like Sam's*.

While Declan looked left at Miss, Rocco took the rubber from Declan's pencil-case. Rocco scrubbed at the smudges but it made them worse. Each stroke made a black line and left a dirty little worm of rubber on the page. He tried blowing but the worms were stuck there and when Rocco swiped at them, they left more dirty streaks.

'That's my rubber,' Declan screamed like he'd been hit.

Miss frowned, her eyes on Rocco. She set Sam's book in front of him and rubbed his floppy hair, all washed and brushed, all perfect, as usual. Miss let out a sigh and came around the table.

Rocco threw Declan's rubber behind him and he imagined it bouncing its way across the classroom floor like a skimmer stone at the ponds.

'Miss, he threw it on the floor!' Declan's face was like a squashed sponge and Rocco was sure water would come out of it.

Rocco hated Declan. He hated them all.

'Pick that up,' said Miss.

'I didn't do it,' said Rocco, arms and head raised to the ceiling.

'Rocco, go pick it up, now. Make the right choice.'

'It wasn't even me,' Rocco said, and pushed his sheet away from him. He got up and looked around. 'I can't even see it,' he said.

He saw Miss reach for his drawing and before he knew it, Rocco had grabbed it and crumpled it into a ball.

'Rocco, why are you like… Rocco, sit back on your seat,' said Miss, her voice in her throat.

Rocco threw the paper in the bin and went to his seat.

'Class, we don't give Rocco any attention when he's behaving like this,' Miss said, like Rocco wasn't even there. She walked to her desk and on the way stopped at the bin and took out Rocco's work. She flattened it out then held it up for everyone to see.

The class giggled. She shouldn't be allowed to do this to him. He would get her back.

'Declan did it,' Rocco said. 'He smudged it all.'

'No, I didn't Miss,' said Declan, 'he's lying.'

'No, *he's* lying,' Rocco shouted and pushed Declan who flew forward whacking his elbow off the desk.

'Awoah,' Declan cried out and then the water came.

Mammy was right, Rocco thought. Cry babies *are* annoying. You shouldn't cry, ever. And if you really have to, do it where no-one can see.

'That's a red card,' said Miss. 'Time Out Table. Now!'

Miss hated Rocco. He knew it. He didn't care, though. He hated her too.

Rocco sat in the dark corner of the classroom beside the bookshelves. He looked at the three large egg timers on the table. He watched Miss as she bent down over Declan and hugged him. Whispered to him. She never hugged Rocco. Or whispered.

'How long, Miss?' Rocco asked.

'Turn over the red timer,' she said, without looking up.

Rocco spun the giant timer. 5 minutes. He looked at the walls. There was the numeracy display with clocks they'd made as homework, telling time at quarter past and to. Some had used coloured card to cut out clock hands that were tacked in the centre with shiny silver pins. Who had things like that at home? Rocco had drawn the time on a digital clock face. Miss said that was very good, really original but not what she'd asked them to do. She didn't put Rocco's up on the display because she'd said, you couldn't change his time, his clock was set forever and besides no-one could play with it, it wasn't interactive.

Rocco looked at the Extra Homework display where the smart ones, the posh ones, had done stuff they didn't even have to. He'd only done extra homework once after they'd been to Belfast Zoo. He didn't have any colouring pencils at home but you could still see it was a peacock, you just had to add the colour inside your head. He knew how to do this because he had to with the TV at home after Mammy fell on her way to bed and knocked it over. It had been black and white ever since. Rocco wondered if the others could do what he could, make magic inside his head, and wanted to show them all his special talent but he just couldn't seem to find a way of letting them see it.

The zoo was the best day of his life even though it had rained and he'd had no coat. He didn't have a packed lunch either but to be fair his mammy didn't really know he was going. He'd hounded her for the trip money, begged and begged, but she wasn't made of money, she'd said. He forged her signature on the permission slip after he'd gotten the money for helping out Mr Salmon from down the street.

The whole zoo was built on a hill and they walked up it looking at the animals. Miss allowed the class to go off on their own but everyone wanted to be with her. They hung from every limb, like monkeys. She held their hands, making sure they all got a turn holding some of her. She let them lean against her on the bench. She even let some hug her.

When Miss ran up the hill, they all ran with her. She stopped at an enclosure, pointed out some animal hiding in the bushes. Miss read the sign telling all about what it ate and where it was from but Rocco couldn't even see it. He went off on his own. Miss shouted for him to stay near, where she could see him.

Rocco wasn't really interested in the animals, he studied the people. He saw mummies and daddies with their wee ones. Saw how they talked to each other and pointed at things together, sort of like Miss and his class. He saw a mum and dad with their little boy and he wished there was a sign about them, telling what they ate and where they were from.

The daddy knew all about everything. And had snacks in his pocket. Daddy unwrapped a fruit bar thing Rocco had never even seen before and Rocco thought he knew every sweet. The wrapper said *organic with no added sugar*. He was going to eat one of those one day. He couldn't see the name but he'd remember the crocodile on the wrapper. He'd steal it if he had to because it wasn't even fair some people had things that other people didn't, especially when it's not even their own fault they don't!

He saw the kid's shoes. They weren't cool. Thick and leather and instead of holes where you put laces through there were little metal hooks. Like boots mountaineers wear. Rocco had seen them on the TV. There was no way this boy was a mountaineer - his mummy and daddy wouldn't let him, it was too dangerous a thing for this little boy to do. But he could probably be, a mountaineer, when he grew up, if he wanted. He was the kind of boy who could be anything he wanted.

The mummy looked at Rocco and smiled. She was the most beautiful woman he'd ever seen, after

Miss, so he smiled at her eyes, the way he'd practiced, and pretended he was a good boy.

The mummy nodded to Rocco, put her hand on her son's shoulders and guided him up the hill. Daddy, of course, followed. They stopped together at the lions.

Rocco made his way over too and stood beside them. He stared at the mummy and when she looked, he tried his smile one more time and she smiled back, but not with the same smile as before.

'Who are you with?' the mummy asked.

'Rocco,' Miss shouted from behind him.

Rocco looked over at Miss coming towards them.

'I'm sorry,' Miss said, 'is he bothering you?'

'No, it's fine. We were just worried,' the mummy lied. She was just like all the rest.

'Come on Rocco,' Miss raised her hand and went for his shoulder but stopped just above it, floating.

Rocco shook his shoulder like he didn't want her to touch him and headed off on his own.

She didn't even try to stop him. He even walked slowly too. 'Don't go far, Rocco,' she called after, when he got far enough away.

He marched up the hill til he was out of breath to show Miss and the mummy just how much he didn't care about them.

Indian Peacock it said at the enclosure. Rocco looked around the inside but saw nothing. He read the sign... *also found in Sri Lanka and other parts of eastern Asia...famous tail plumage...bright, blue heads and crest colourings...*

There was nothing even in the enclosure. *This*

zoo was crap, he decided and kicked the chain-link fence. He hoped people had seen. That he would get in trouble. *Let them come and shout. What were they gonna do?* He kicked again. And again. The fencing warping, carrying the metallic wave along.

Movement on the right. This jerking bird-animal. Rocco looked to see if anyone else saw it but he was alone. The family he'd stood beside were coming up the hill. He didn't want to be near them again but there was only one way back down, past them, so he stood, staring at the peacock.

The peacock turned towards Rocco then froze. It had seen him, Rocco was sure. More, it was staring at him. Rocco stared back. Its head had little stalks, in a line, sticking into the air with what looked like tiny blue flowers on top. Like an American Indian headdress.

At first, he thought the peacock was wearing a coat, or a beautiful cloak like Joseph's, Miss had read them the story in circle time. He saw it wasn't a cloak, but the peacock's tail that trailed along the ground behind, a multi-coloured wedding train.

The peacock came towards him. Straight over and no mistaking. It was staring right into Rocco's eyes, he could feel it. The peacock, and he knew how stupid this sounded, the peacock… liked him. He just knew. His inside told him.

Rocco felt the family next to him. He heard his class coming up the hill but didn't look anywhere but straight ahead at the peacock because they were… friends. And they weren't going to let anyone else in. He heard his class arrive, talking about his peacock, whether it would show its special tail. They made kissing sounds, calling the peacock to them, trying to steal it away from Rocco, take his friend away. *Didn't they have enough? All of them. Couldn't they let him have this one thing?*

But the peacock didn't look at anyone else no matter what sounds they made or if they were teacher's pet or even if they had mountaineer's shoes.

And neither did Rocco.

And while his class all made noise, Rocco stayed silent.

'He's staring at you, Rocco,' said Miss.

She could see. They all could see. *Show them,* Rocco thought to the peacock. *Show them all how amazing you are. For me.*

And it did. The peacock raised its tail. Bustled and shook, with the sound of a sudden wind through leaves, it spread its beautiful blue for him. And this small thing became huge, though its body stayed the same size, it took up ten times the space.

'Wow,' he heard. 'Look at that,' they said, pushing against the fence. All wide eyes on the peacock like they were watching magic, or fireworks.

On its feathers there were eyes. Eyes all over the tail. Looking at his class who thought they were the ones looking.

It was all everyone talked about on the bus back to school. Rocco's peacock. They tried to find a new nickname for him. A funny one. Not like what they usually called him. None of the new nicknames were any good. None stuck.

He drew the picture at home that night and brought it into school the next day. Miss put it up on the Extra Homework wall. If he'd had coloured pencils at home, to really show the peacock, he knew, things would have been different from that day on. But, so what? Anyway, he could see the colours on his drawing, even though it was in black and white. Only he could.

'Rocco is your time up?' Miss asked.

Rocco turned away from his drawing and looked at Miss. He looked at the timer. It had finished. He hadn't noticed. He went over to the Extra Homework wall, ripped his drawing from the board, its corners stayed behind attached to the tacks that had held it up.

'Rocco,' Miss called.

He looked at his drawing.

'Rocco what are you doing? Make the right choice,' she said.

Rocco looked at her. At the Behaviour Chart behind her.

'Make the right choice,' she said, walking towards him.

He held his picture up to show everyone.

'Rocco don't. Don't do it, Rocco.'

He ripped his drawing.

'Not your lovely drawing, Rocco.'

He looked at her. She seemed like she really meant it. So he tore a long strip.

'Rocco, remember the peacock? Remember how he looked at you that day. Only you,' Miss said. 'You all remember?'

'Yes, Miss,' said the class.

He looked at them. Silent and staring. All those eyes.

He tore another strip. And again. His picture now long tails hanging flat from his hand. Rocco was smiling, but not like they do, not with his lips.

He looked at Miss. She was really looking at him. They all were.

Do I Know You?
by
Elizabeth Reapy

Candlelight flickers in the space between us and I'm sweating. It's not my first romance, I had a girlfriend when I was younger and I've obviously gone for pints before but I never done this fancy restaurant jazz. I've never met up with someone since moving into the city. Since the incident with my sister. I take off the navy lambswool jumper, reveal the checked royal blue shirt underneath. Both borrowed from Dessie in the hostel. He has this thing about looking smart, even if everything else about him lets him down - the smell, the slurring of words, bloodshot eyes - he'll be wearing neat clothes.

I can't decipher if my date is nervous, she says very little but she could be a quiet one. Her make-up is heavy, theatrical almost, in this light. Her eyes have all these black shadows around them but don't seem as melancholy in real life as they did in her pictures. 'Where do you work?' she asks.

I know she's on the line in the American plant that makes little metal pieces to keep rich people's hearts open. She told me in a text, fumed about the rush hour traffic. I remember scrolling through her message and looking out onto the road, at the line of cars bumper to bumper, exhaust pipes leaking gloomy air. My breath misted in front of my face as I sat on an old fleece blanket, coffee cup in my other hand. I wondered if she was in one of the cars and how often might strangers pass before they meet?

I scratch my neck and then my chin. 'Fundraising,' I say, wave it off. 'We're out, let's not discuss the office.'

She presses her lips together, nods. The restaurant is packed with glossy brown tables and white candles and couples. A harpist strums in the corner. There's a waft of fish and perfume but that could be from the ones across from us. The woman's bangles jingle as she slices strips of lettuce, and her partner, after devouring a huge piece of trout, picks fine bones from his tongue.

Silence grasps as I search for something to say. Thankfully, the waitress comes to take our orders.

'Do I know you?' the waitress asks. She's dark eyed and dark haired. Spanish or Italian maybe.

I barely glance at her, mumble, 'No.' She couldn't know me. No way. When I'm tapping, I wear a scarf over my mouth, a cap pulled down over my face. Nobody'd recognise me, if they were to come from home. My sister wouldn't notice me. And my father, well, he's not ever going to be out and about again. I blink hard, squashing the image of his thinning body, his morphine drip.

I fumble with the wine menu and my fingers leave clammy prints on the plastic.

The waitress touches her hairband. 'I never forget a face. I know you from somewhere.'

My head's still shaking. Just ignore her. She doesn't. She couldn't. I point at the menu. My sponsor will kill me. 'Zinfandel. The bottle. Please.'

I don't want to be cheap and mention the prices right now, but there's a sting happening here, and I'd know. I'm using sting money to pay for the evening. The new jeans from the shopping centre and the suede loafers from the second-hand. I'd sold coke to some British tourists and a hen party, and by coke I mean paracetamol from the pharmacy cut with a salt sachet and wrapped in the jacks of Supermac's. The hens were drunk out of it, wasted, they wouldn't notice and the tourists, it's hard for me to pretend to care about them. A handy 200 euro to cover the food, this bottle and a generous tip for the waitress, if she'd stop being so intense. She gazes at me, hums a little, as she taps our order into a small machine in her palm.

I take a deep breath in through my nose.

'You remind me of someone as well,' my date says.

'No,' I say, too quickly, as if to command her to stop.

'The American singer J-Den, do you know him?'

I shake my head, relief causes me to grin.

'What type of music do you like?' she asks.

I scrape my mind for an answer. 'Trad is okay. I hear it a lot, well since moving here, and now I don't mind it.'

Her mouth is tight again. I look at the brass handles on the front door of the restaurant. The street outside is different shades of gray as the sun sinks.

After a few moments, my date picks up her fork and traces the place mat with it. 'I quite like J-Den. His new album is fun.'

The waitress returns and pours a dribble of the wine into my glass.

'You can keep going.' I urge her to add more.

'No, you must sample, see if it's to your liking.'

I take a little sip. It tastes like wine. 'Perfectly delightful,' I say in an accent and gesture again for more. My date smiles and her gums show.

The waitress fills my date's glass and stares at me again. An uncomfortable jabbing starts in my guts. She places the bottle beside the candle.

'Did we meet at Heart Gathering?' she asks.

'At what?' I say, leave my mouth open.

'Heart Gathering, the spiritual festival in Sligo. Were you one of the healers?'

I laugh hard. Jesus. Of all the things I'd been called in my life, this was a new one. 'No, I haven't a notion on what a Heart Gathering is.'

'Very well,' she says, 'my apologies.'

When the waitress is out of earshot, I say 'Sounds daft,' to my date. She giggles. 'The wine's good, yeah?'

She sips and nods, before she's even swallowed.

I wipe my forehead with the back of my hand, take a big mouthful and I feel the liquid swarm through my body. Exhaling deeply, I wonder if things are going to be okay after all, like Dessie's always telling me.

'You must know J-Den?'

I shake my head. 'No clue.'

My date doesn't seem to care that I don't care about this singer. She drinks quickly and tells me details of how he raps too, where his songs went in the charts, some of his rivals. My thoughts drift to Heart Gathering. The waitress with her hair loose, wearing yoga pants, holding hands and chanting peace and love in some healing circle.

She interrupts my daydream by placing my meal in front of me. The slow roasted beef rib is a bone poking upwards from a hunk of meat. There's a side scoop of mash and carrots and some herbs artily placed in the centre of the plate. My date has gone for poached salmon.

The waitress lingers, 'Need anything else?'

I've my cutlery in hand, ready to tuck in.

'It's just,' she says and pauses. 'I never forget a face. It's bothering me now. I know you from somewhere.'

I give her a sorry-can't-help-you sort of a shrug and gulp some of the saliva that's gathering in my cheeks. Guilty sensations prick my body. But what am I supposed to do here? I'm on a fucking evening out. I'm trying to be normal.

My date helps herself to another glass and skulls it. Maybe we do have something in common. She tells me more about J-Den - his romantic life now. He's been spotted on a beach in the Maldives with a blondie one from a reality TV show. She's got a fake arse.

'A fake arse? What does that mean?'

'She got implants put in. They used fat from her belly and silicone, filled up her cheeks to round them out.'

'That's mad,' I say, slice some more meat away from the bone.

I zone out and finish my meal. The portion was tiny. Another sting. I cross the fork over the knife, to show I'm done and the sweat ices on the back of my neck.

Maybe she actually does know me.

The waitress, has she cleared my plate before? I see her in her hippie gear, volunteering at the soup kitchen. She's one of the pretty foreign ones. A plastic apron over her yoga pants. She always smiles and tries to engage in small talk. I never chat to anyone, just get the meal, wolf it and leave but I don't wear my disguise in there either.

She's going to remember me.

I glance at the clock in the corner. My dates picks away at her dinner and continues her soliloquy about the singer's lifestyle.

I say, 'I've to leave,' and rapidly gesture to catch the waitress's attention.

'Excuse me?' my date says.

'I've to head,' I say, still waving at the waitress. 'Can we get the bill?'

'You can't go,' my date says and points her fork at her plate. 'I'm still eating.'

'It's been nice. I'll get this.'

'Don't – you can't go,' my date says, she looks winded.

The waitress goes to the cash register, comes over with the bill wallet and two imperial mints on a plate. 'All okay?'

I check it, take the ball of cash out of my pocket and peel notes in. I give her a fiver tip and my chair makes a scraping sound as I push it back.

'Bye,' I say, smiling.

'Wait,' the waitress shouts after me. 'I remembered.'

As I rush away, she reaches for my arm and turns me to face her. My heart plummets thinking of the friary's free lunches. Will she tell my date and all these fancy fuckers who eat here on the regular where I usually eat?

Maybe I should own it. Shout it myself. 'I kept stealing my dad's cancer drugs. My sister caught me and instead of slapping me, instead of saying I was not to be trusted around my father, she apologised. Sorry she didn't look after me enough when I was younger.' My eyes burn and shame flares through my body at the memory of it.

The waitress says, 'You look like the rapper, J-Den. I mixed you up with him,' and she cracks a beautiful smile.

'Oh.'

I leave the restaurant and scratch the gap where my beard doesn't quite meet my hairline. I suppose I could go back in now. Sit with my date while she finishes. No. It's done. It's over. It was a stupid notion anyway. The whole thing. Who was I kidding? The breeze on my face is like a gift. I run through the square, back to the hostel and hope to sneak in past everyone but Dessie spots me dashing by the TV room.

He summons me. 'Come on, young fella, we know you're a gent but tell us something. We're all wondering.'

I pick fluff off the jumper he loaned me. 'Yeah. Lovely time. Yep.'

He whoops. 'Glad to hear it. Meeting a good girl. You're on your way again. Soon you'll get yourself back onto your college course. Do great things with your life.'

I smirk and slip away to the dorm.

Nobody's in. It's been cleaned but the room has a smell of old socks. I lay on my bunk, sighing. Why do I always run? Why is that always the only response I have to anything? The impulse to leg it. Run. Go.

I think about texting my date but instead I Google J-Den. He's got porcelain like teeth and bleached hair. His shirt is open in every picture, chest and abs so defined, they could be drawn on. Even when I squint I look nothing like him. And there's your woman, fake arse, with soft blonde flowing hair like waves, similar megawatt teeth. She's shaped like a Barbie. They hold hands as they look out to the turquoise sea. I could run and join in on their date, sit on the white sand, coconut sunblock all over me. Sell them a wrap made from a sachet of Supermac's salt and paracetamol, charge them French restaurant prices for it.

My face is wet and I didn't even notice. I press my cheeks and think about spending the rest of the cash on a six pack, a bottle of Bucky, whatever drugs are going, fuck off to oblivion. Could text one of the boys, someone will definitely be downtown causing trouble.

Just stay.

A voice says, it's a low voice but clear as clean water. There's no one in the room. I look around, spooked. I press the screen off and catch my reflection in the black mirror of the phone.

Stay.

Black is the Colour
by
Dave Lordan

TURN DOWN THE MUSIC I SAID TURN DOWN
THE FUCKIN MUSIC. C'mon lads. Shush will ye?
Actually I'm goin to turn the music off, turn it right
fuckin off for a minute actually, right? Pass me the end
o' that joint Slev will ya, till I tell ye me story. I wanna
tell ye this story, this story here, before we put on the
next song cos I luv this song an I luv it cos of this ting,
this stupid oul' ting that happened to me donkey's years'
ago in Lungdung. So listen up the lot o' yis, will yis?

So I'm standin on me tod outside Victoria Cross train
station sometime before Christmas in 1981. I know it
was nineteen-eighty-one because there's loads a fuckin
republican stuff goin on. Marchin, riots, snipers, all that
shite. The hunger strikes, remember? Bobby Sands an all
that. I'm standin there just waitin for me bus to come
along. I'd a few jars in me too. Wen don't I? I'm standin
there an next ting this wan sidles up besides me an says
'are ya lookin for a trick luv'? Jaysus ya should o' seen
the state of her lads. Withered, fuckin ruined man, dats
all I'll say, fuckin shrivelled. She could of been twenty-
five. She could of been fifty-five. An she still out there
workin' man. Fair play to her in one way, ya know what
I mean? Anyways I didn't want any trick so I just says 'I
don't want any trick off ya luv' Fuckin stoopid word for
it it ain't it? Trick me bollix. As if she was gonna whip
out a deck of cards or a fuckin top hat with a rabbit in it.

46

So enannyways she gets the hump or doesn't catch me right or watever an she's scowlin at me an says 'ya a fuckin queer or somethink a fuckin oirish fuckin queer ?'. 'No' I said, 'take it feckin aisy', I said. 'Howld yar horses', I said. 'Didn't mean to offend ya an what not.' 'Sometin fuckin wrong with me den, is it? Don't like the look of me or somethink?' she asks me. I can smell the ale off her now ya know, smell the rot. She's like a rag-doll lads. Like sometin ya'd throw out in a skip golluvus. My heart's goin out to her. Twould make ya fuckin weep to look at her. 'Nothin wrong with ya love. Nothin atall' . 'Go on den' says she. 'What kind of trick ya into den?'. an I just says I wouldn't disrespec ya luv. I don't do tricks with no-one. I'll talk to ya no problem, though. Why don't we just have a little chat like?

An den she softens a bit an says 'Go on talk to me den Oirish. I love that Oirish accent. Could listen to it all day, if I'd the fuckin time'. an I says to her d'ya mind if I go an get a cup of coffee luv?

An den she softens a bit an says 'Go on talk to me den Oirish. I love that Oirish accent. Could listen to it all day, if I'd the fuckin time'. an I says to her d'ya mind if I go an get a cup of coffee luv? 'Ah ya're just walkin away from me now says she. Ya prick. Go on fuck off den, Oirish cunt'. I put me hands up to calm her an says I wouldn't walk away from ya luv. I woudn't walk away from ya. No way would I walk away from ya. Just a bit cold that's all, a cup a coffee, warm our fuckin hands up at least. Get fuckin frostbite hangin around here. 'Tell me about it' says she 'Tell me about it mate'.

So I skidaddled up to the cafe on the corner an I bought two coffees off an nice Indian chap an went back down to her an she's waitin an den the two of us sat down on the footpath wiv our backs to the station wall an we started nattin together. Usual shite, family an origins, an future fuckin plans an all dat. An all the gawkers lookin at us walkin by. But I didn't give a fuck about people gawkin an o' course she didn't. People gawkin at her all day long I suppose. What was her name now. I'm tryin to think of it. Julie I'll call her. I'm not sure what it was but Julie will do. We all deserve a fuckin name at least don't we, no matter how bad or badly off we are, even if it's the wrong fuckin name? an I told her where I was from an she told me where she was from, Durham it was, coal land, 'coal in the lungs an glue up the fuckin nose' she says.

She told me that she was in Lungdung for years, said she didn't care to remember how many. Said she'd wan daughter, almost a grown up, an she saw her occasionally. She was beautiful this little girl of hers, beautiful supposed to be. an I believed her, about her beautiful daughter, but she could have been makin dat up ya know, people do dat. I do it meself sometimes.

An after a while I asked her if I could put my arm around her . An she said ya go on, den. We were sharin a cigarette at the time an when I passed her the fag I threw my arm around her shoulder an I pulled her in a bit closer to me an it was a good idea because it was cold an dark now like it gets in the evenin times in winter in

Lungdung. an den this feelin came over me an I wanted to sing. I just had to sing like. I had to sing to her. an I said do ya mind if i sing to ya? an she said 'Not at all Oirish not atall. I'd like that. Sin me a song, den'. an I sang her this song lads an I'll put it on the stereo now for ye after I give ye the first few lines. Are ye listening? Right. This is the song I sang for Julie the beaten oul sex worker outside Victoria station as I waited for the bus in the hungry dyin divilfilled year of 1981:

'Black is the colour of my true love's hair,
Her lips are like some roses fair,
She had the sweetest smile an the gentlest hands,
an I Love the ground whereon she stands'

Johnny And The Lantern
by
Declan O'Rourke

On the road outside of Delvin,
In the shadow of the trees
A man drew out his pistol
and a man fell to his knees,
Well the man who did the shooting,
didn't stick around
But he went and told the others
where the body could be found

Well the saw ripped through his flesh,
but to cut the bones was hell,
Though the blade was old and rusty,
through the bones you couldn't tell,

Well they hacked his legs in pieces,
someone let out a cry,
Johnny hold the lantern,
Johnny hold that up there boy,

Well Johnny's hands were freezing
but he held the lantern high,
As the dead man lay there gazing
and the flame danced in his eye,

Well they cursed his broken body
and with the last strokes of the saw,
As Johnny held the lantern
they cut the hands of law,
Then they buried all the pieces
and their energy was spent,
And the last thing that they buried
was the hands that took the rent,

Well the saw ripped through his flesh
but to cut the bones was hell
Though the blade was old and rusty
through the bones you couldn't tell

On the road outside of Delvin,
at the ditch just round the bend,
Where the trees mar all the moonlight,
that's where Manning met his end.

This song is from the album "Chronicles Of The Great Irish Famine".

How I Discovered Rhyme
by
Paula Meehan

Not long back from London
my father had done a deal with a man
key money down on a house
in Bargy Road, East Wall,
an illegal corporation tenancy
in those days of no work, no roof,
no hope, no time like the present
to come home with three small children
and another on the way to what

was familiar at least. Dublin rain
and Dublin roads and Dublin streets
and Dublin pubs and Dublin pain.
May blossom in the park and empty pockets.

I think it was then my mother gave up:
pre-natal, post-natal who knows now.
They are so young, my mother and father,
to me who has grown old

in their light, in their shade.
They have too much on their plate —
including Ucker Hyland's chickens.
Part of the deal for the house
was to mind this man's chickens.
He kept them in the back yard
in makeshift crates and lofts.
Sporadically he'd deliver sacks of feed.

We'd have pots of popcorn every night
to Felix the Cat and to Bolek and Lolek
and the birth pangs of Irish Television.

We settled in. We fed the hens.
The man came. He took the eggs.
He'd wring the odd neck.
He wore two overcoats
belted by a length of rope.
And then a letter: the Eviction Notice.
Some neighbour had ratted us out.
There were rows, recriminations,
slammed doors, my father silent.

The stay in Bargy Road ended
on a bitter winter's day,
the Tolka low and the tang of rot.
We came home from school to bailiffs
boarding up the windows, to all
we had on show in the garden,
paltry in the dying light —
a few sticks of furniture,
the mattress with its shaming stain
nearly the shape of Ireland,
the Slot TV, our clothes in pillowcases
and our Christmas dolls grubby
and inadequate on the grass.

My mother was frantically chasing the
chickens;
we put down our satchels and joined in.
My father was gone for the lend

of a van or a cart. The street-lights
came on and here comes
the henman around the corner —

Ucker Hyland! Ucker Hyland!
coats flapping and oaths spitting from his big
lips
and all of us then round and round the garden
the winter stars come out and
feathers like some angelic benison
settling kindly on all that we owned.

From 'Troika', *Painting Rain,* Carcanet Press,
Manchester, 2009.

By Chris Agee

The Rainbow Poem

Well, when we finally came back again, there
it was: *the cypress absence,* ramifying. But some days
later, something else happened: a rainbow arcing
over Brdo and our now-solo cypress, for
the first time ever (for us). As if clarifying
the beauties of absence. Like the one
in "The Village" the afternoon of Miriam's death
when hailstones darkened our windshield for good.

The Cypress Poem

Yes, we lost that second cypress to the saw
of an idiot neighbour: an immense squarish one,

                                        paired with ours
like an old couple reaching across an untended wall.
                                           But soon enough
I saw three other smaller cypress above another neighbours
stone-roofed shed, like slim arrowheads or svelte swords
I had never thought about or dwelt upon. A lesson in itself:
vistas of incremental change after a great clean-cut change.

The Dove Poem

Because we were late, or later, neither
the golden oriole nor the blue-fronted jays, almond-seeking,
came this year – but something else did
come: the beautiful doves, in a heart-flutter
and flurry of purplegrey and white insignia flashing
in flocks over rooftops under gloomy cloud …
Lesson? *Listen*: It's Vojka's oft-times
Always expect the unexpected. Like the small
perfect cat that walked into the night – and never
came back. Or this, the poem.

Žrnovo, Croatia, September-October 2021

Some Arabs Are Blue-Eyed
by
Alan Morrison

The Street Arabs are camping out in Bognor
Rolling out their cardboard carpets on the pavements
Of the pedestrianised street, grime-singed white rags
Wrapped round their heads like makeshift keffiyeh
To keep them cool, damp out the pounding sun;
Some improvise tents out of deconstructed boxes,
Sleeping bags for back-props like camel saddles
With canvas pads as makeshift chairs, or head-props;
Some bear complexions of burnt orange, others
Of leathery brown, they don't want to get too
Tanned in case they rub the Bognor 'Gammon'
Up the wrong way, whose umbrages are terrible,
Who labour under make believe that 'Brexit' has banished
All immigrants, refugees, and beggarly Arabs;
Not Ali Baba but Al the Barber and his red-and-white-
Striped pole signposting he's open for business once
The klaxon announces Close Sesame on incomers,
And Britain's cast itself adrift and 'taken back control',
At least then the street Arabs will all be Caucasians,
Many with eyes deep blue as their black passports -
Black or blue, it's disputable, a moot point open to
Perceptions - but we digress as we regress, let us stress:
Henceforth it'll be British streets for *British* homeless...

Previously published in *The Morning Star*

Scot of the Car Park
by
Alan Morrison

He's bedded in now for the cutting winter
Encamped in frozen eiderdowns and sleeping bags
Frostbitten eyes blinking through the slit
In his Balaclava helmet, he's almost as stiff
As a post at his outpost just off the high street
Part-insulated from biting winds
By iron bars that mark the boundary
Of the supermarket car park -that's his pitch,
Tent of tarpaulin, swears he's not outside alone,
That ghosts of old companions shadow
Him everywhere, ubiquitous at this altitude,
Shadows hovering through the snow
Of solipsistic shoppers in consumerist tundra -
He needs a pee but he's too cold to climb out
From his snowed-in dug-out, he knows
If he does he'll be gone for some time,
Could get lost, or be bruised blue as his lips,
Crushed ice to soothe the bumps, might not be
Able to find his way back, so best keep
The small plastic Union Jack fluttering
From the top of his crumpled mound before
It freezes over and is polished to an igloo,
An iced dome, a chill booth, a frosted tomb,
Him a frozen adult foetus inside a frigid womb...

Previously published in *Poetry and All That Jazz*

The Pigeon Spikes
by
Alan Morrison

Pigeons perch on the scrawny shoulders
And bony elbows of the *Big Issue* vendor
Who pitches outside the supermarket
Near where unsponsored rough sleepers
Mutely appeal with cupped hands or empty
Cardboard Costa Coffee cups for pennies
In spite of Public Space Protection Orders,
And fly defiantly in the face of "*defensive
Architecture*": buildings fortified
With metal studs cemented like gummed
Teeth to deter human vertebrae, while
Bus stops are benchless but for narrow
Sloping plastic bum-perches, and park
Benches are newly segmented by iron
Arm-rests to guard against vagrants
Lying down to get some shut-eye…

The vendor thinks, if only he could pull in
As many punters as pigeons that settle on
The spindly perches of his shoulders;
If only his palms filled up with pound coins
As much as with crumbs for pecking beaks
Of cooing columbiformes; but then
This is his special gift from the grit of circumstance:
To be a living statue for pigeons to perch on…

But it can only be a matter of time until
This curious purpose turns metamorphosis:

For rumours moot the homeless are now
Little more than anthropomorphised pigeons,
Discouraged from roosting at night in sheltered
Entrance-ways or porches to posh apartments
By the sprouting of small metal spikes,
Blunt-tipped but thoroughly uncomfortable,
Knobbly to the back if one was to sprawl
Upon them for an acupunctural nap,
Spine-nudging studs, beds of blunt nails,
The most literal of blunt instruments,
Toothed oysters, fold-out Lilo iron maidens —
(Though better by far than being tipped out
Into rubbish crunchers from Biffa bins);
Similar to those spikes put on tops of railings
To send out clear messages to winging pigeons
Not to perch there on pain of being impaled —
Not so much a '*hand up*' as a spike up
That place where the sun don't shine! *Look,*
People: pigeon spikes to repel rough sleepers!
Not so much as a coo from the popular press —
Just ricocheting "*Scrounger*" quips from the *Express*…

So man and pigeon cooperate, homeless
Homo sapien and proscribed columbiforme
Pitch in together, sculpt out a strange
Familiar solidarity: human head
And shoulders for perches, mangy pigeon
Plumage for feathered umbrellas… (*Now only*
Shadows get heads down under porches)…

From *Shabbigentile* (Culture Matters, 2019)

Ballad of a Drunk Man
by
Gerard Lee

On high stools tight to the bar
Twitchy men arrange their wallet junk,
Or feign an appetite for stale news
In old papers yellowing under charity cans
They often think of stealing.

Fuck the poor he slurs and hurls the cordial decanter
Shattering a plate glass mirror
Like it's ice between him and his next drink.
Barman and bouncer pinball him out
Into the blinding day.

Red-faced by the early house
He smokes. Graceless delirium
Of his tremens hand drags long
On a cadged butt, inhalation's grimace
His morning's work.

Whiskey stripped him of all that counted
Right down to the light in his eye,
Left him stravaging about
In old bursted Reeboks

Unrecognizable.
To all that is, but death,
Who follows him everywhere now
Waiting for him to finish up.

Tommo, A few lines
by
Karl Parkinson

I was born in Saint Matthews Gardens, in 1985, yeah, actually born right there in the flats, ma's waters broke on the stairs of the block, and with the help of Mrs. Daley, who had fourteen children of her own, and knew all about givin birth, little Tommo stuck his head out into an inner city Dublin with smog filled skies, junkies all over the place, every second cunt was on the dole, joyridin was big time, and what the papers these days call *Gangland* culture was in full flow, I'd say the first sounds I heard were sirens, and singin, and children's street games.

Me aulone, Annie has worked as an office cleaner, a bar lady, a waitress, all sorts, when she's not on the scratcher of course, me aulfella, Kevin was a drunk, a gambler, a pick pocket, used to bate me ma, and all of us, served time in prison on 3 occasions, the longest he done was 6 years for GBH and robbery, he was only five foot six, and weighed 150 lbs soakin wet with rocks in his pockets as he would say, but the little bastard had a rage worthy of Zeus, capable of extreme violence at any moment, brutal gifts bestowed upon him by the hands of the catholic church, a garda named Killer Kilroy, and the staff at saint marks school for boys, his favourite form of attack was to strike fast and hard with his small hatchet he kept inside his old brown duffle coat.

When I was a younfella, I was in awe and terrified of me da. I'll never forget the first time I saw him beat me ma, five years old I was, Kevin came in drunk, after spendin all his "wages" on drink and horses, Annie kicked up a fuss, Kevin replied with a ferocious attack, punchin and kickin her, takin her by the hair and smashin her head against the wall, stompin her on the ground, leavin her face so badly bruised and swollen that she couldn't leave the flat for three days, for fear of her neighbours seein her, and her body so smashed up, that she could do nothin but lay in bed for days, drinkin only water, and cups of instant chicken soup, that Kevin made her, his way of sayin sorry. I stood by the bed lookin at her, strokin her hair.

Lucy, me sister is younger than me, single mother of three kids from two different fellas, loves a few bottles, loves a take-away, and loves all of us in the family, and me older brother Paul works as a taxi driver, a wife, 3 kids, and a tendency to spend much of his time in the bookies and boozer, follows Liverpool FC, watches horse racin, boxin, rugby, darts and snooker, him and me don't talk much, birthdays, Christenings, funerals, Christmas, Paul never approved of me lifestyle, or me drug takin, but the prick doesn't mind gettin a nice bag of Charlie for him and his pals when they're away for a "Golf weekend." See in Dublin, heroin and crack is bad, but coke and weed and vodka is all grand, yuh know?

I hung around with Raymond Cassidy since we were little, Rayo and me playin football, and chasin, and other kids games in the block, robbin from shops, and gettin into fights with other lads from the flats in St Matthews and other flats around Dublin, smokin and drinkin on Halloween, stealin cars and joyridin on the pitch of the flats, doin time in borstal, sellin hash, rippin off hippies for fake E's in town, batterin rivals, runnin a small crew, goin to proper jail, sellin gear and coke, runnin thins on the small north-side patch we had.

I had me first wet dream when I was nine, a voluptuous, blonde women, naked, with big breasts. I told Raymond about it in the garden that day, and me ma heard us, and said don't be talkin about dirty stuff like that. I had me first wank at 10, but it was just a little piss horn, the first time I came proper was when I wanked to a picture of a black women on the ten of diamonds of me uncle George's porno cards that he brought back from Spain, I robbed her from the pack, and brought her to the bathroom, and had it out there in the sink.

The first real porn I seen was when I was 13 and was in James Ganning's gaff, with Rayo, Trevor Mackie, and Blob Sullivan, Blob had gotten a hold of a video of a full porn movie, it was made in 1979 and all the blokes in it had moustaches, and the woman had full bushes and some of them looked no better than the aulones in the block, we watched it, laughin, smilin, awkward, hard dicks in our wet pants, when Raymond finally got up and said I'm goin for a wank in yer jacks James, everyone laughed, and one by one we went in had quick wanks, into James's toilet and sink, him shoutin fuckin clean up after yiz, me Aul fella will kill me if someone's spunk is on his sink or floor.

The first girl I kissed was Linda Sanders, I was 7 and she was 9, she ambushed me with two friends, they swiped me football and ran up the stairs of the block, I chased them, pantin and red faced got to the top of the stairs, the 3 girls were there, the ball behind their backs, waitin like a gang of them prayin mantis yokes I seen on one of them BBC nature docs, to pounce on me, two of them grabbed me by the arms and neck and pushed me into Linda, she threw her arms around me and says Give us a kiss and yuh can have yer ball back, a blushin Tommo here, says OK, I leaned in and kissed Linda on the lips, she tasted like gobstopper sweets, I didn't mind, sure they were me favourite sweets, we kissed again, and then again, and the other girls giggled, and started singin *Tommo loves Linda, Tommo loves Linda*, and Linda said to me, I'm yer girlfriend now, cause we kissed, and I just said OK, cool, and took the ball up under me arm, and we walked back down the stairs together, the girls still singin *Tommo loves Linda, Tommo loves Linda, la la la la la la!*

Sit down, shut up eat yer dinner, be a good boy, do as yer ma tells yuh. Go to school, wear a uniform. Be good in class, put yer hand up. Answer questions correctly like everyone else. Do exercise, jump about, joggin on the spot. Do homework. Be quiet, play football, get yer hair cut short. Wear one earrin in yer ear, drink cider, smoke hash, eat quarter pounders from the chipper, rob cars, beat up strangers. Go to prison, get stabbed, stab someone, throw boilin water in a rats face. Be the man, the fuckin man. The man, the man, the man, the big man, the little man.

Da used to say, Here's the man, now, how's the little man doin today?

Me Da's face hairy, eyes bloodshot. Smellin of tobacco, fingers yellow-brown. Roll ups. Rizla. He told me the rollin papers were flavoured eatin paper, red ones taste like oranges, green ones mint. Not for kids, grown-ups food.

Cud be funny de old man. Cud be a bastard as well. Had hard knotted hands. When he hit yuh could leave a mark on yea for days. Like a birthmark, purple splatter on yer back.

Ma is a slender woman with long fingers, I coulda been a piano player, with these fingers, me old teacher miss Hanlon used to say, imagine that, hah, me playin the piano, fuck sake, what a dream, might have if I never met that bollix in there and got pregnant, only 17 I was, a well, that's life, life...

She would go on like that all the time when talkin to us kids.

Me aul Ma, jaysus the shit we put her through. The aul fella that fucker. Lived in de pub, smoked all day. Came home, shouted, smacked, kicked. We didn't talk to each other all that much.

First memory I have of the aulfella is when I was 3 or 4, playin with a toy tool set, plastic hammers and screwdrivers, sittin there on the floor on an ugly grey carpet with stains on it, the pet Collie dog lappin water from its tray. I'm hammerin away and crash! An ashtray hit the wall about 5 feet from me, fuckin glass and smoke butts flew everywhere. I was shakin and cryin for ages.

The aulfella, for a reason known only to himself, smashed the ashtray off the wall.

The memory is not in black and white, like in the movies when they have some fake arty load of shite and all the flashbacks are in black and white. It's in fuckin bright techno colour HD, I max. The Aulfella died, what is it? Five, no, six years ago now. His liver was fucked, and his lungs, drink and smokes.

School is where I learned how to fight. I learnt by losin fights. I got hit, got beat up,
I survived, bloodied, bruised, but I lived.
I said to meself, not too bad, I can take been hit and Da hit me harder than any one at school.

I lost the fear of been hit and started to hit back.

One day when I was only fourteen I hit the bloke who's supposed to be the best scrapper in school, and was seventeen, so hard and fast that I knocked his tooth out and bust his lip open, right then I became the most feared fighter in the school for about two years, till mad dog Maddox smashed me up one day in the yard, now he's a proper hard cunt, I was relegated to a decent goer, Mad dog was king.

I remember the time when Ma went missin for two weeks, walked out, said she was goin the shop for milk and bread. Came back with a black eye, and a split lip, and da holdin onto her like she was a prize he won or a dog that got off the lead and ran away and was gettin brought back home. She ran off with Paul Mc Dermot, they were seein each other, da found them and sorted it out with a hammer, Mc Dermot was never the same after that, used to be a good lookin bloke. The scar on his head didn't make em so attractive to the ladies anymore and the vacant stare in his eye's scared all the kids in the flats, Zombie Paul we used to call him, he died a few years ago, walked out in front of Hi-ace van and got knocked down, the joke went around that yuh could actually kill a Zombie after all.

Ma wasn't the same either after that day. She hardly left the house much at all, until the aulfella died, then she started to go out to the pub with her sisters, me aunties: Mary, Jacinta, Veronika, and Rose.

Robbin cars was what I first loved to do as a teenager. It gave me a rush. Made yuh feel like the king of the flats.

The buzz was deadly.

The gang that was into robbin cars was, Danny Lennon, Budgie, Mickey Dwyer, Raymond and me. A load of crazy, young, tough and didn't give a fuck youngfellas from the north-side of Dublin. Budgie was the maddest of the lot of us. He was skinny, only 5"4 but would have a go off any one and would use a blade without hesitation, before it became the thing to do like, yuh know?

He would do the craziest things: rob a car across the street from the Bridewell Garda station, Go into shops with a balaclava on and batter the shopkeeper, then rob a few packs of smokes and a bottle of Vodka and leave the money in the till. I'd only buy drink and smokes anyway, he'd say. Danny was a fat fucker, always eatin a burger from the chipper or a bag of chips and a bar of chocolate, could drink more beer than anyone else. Never had a girlfriend for years, he was a virgin till he was 18 when the lads paid Cathy Jones to have sex with him on his birthday night. She did it for a 2 litter and 10 blue; she's dead now, ended up on the gear, OD. Kids found her at the bottom of the stairs in the flats,

Poor bitch, they said.
Stupid cunt, they said.
That's what yuh get isin it? They said.
Another one, gone from that shit, they said.

Mickey was one of the soundest blokes yuh could ever meet, just don't get on the wrong side of em or trouble be comin yer way, quiet but smooth, always got the girl, and Rayo was the best mate I ever had.

The best years of me life was when we were teenagers not givin a bollix, robbin, fightin, moochin birds, gettin mad out of it on drink, hash and pills, sellin some drugs, small time only, havin a great time. Before we got into all that serious love relationships, kids, hard drugs, jail and death. Ah yeah, if I could be anywhere at any time I'd be there now in the block, standin there with me mates, drinkin a flagon of cider, plannin to rob a car.

The first bird that I got me hole off was Susan Power, lovely little thin she was, blonde hair down to her arse, green eyes, nice pair of tits. We were all in Fat Danny's gaff, his Ma was gone away for the weekend, so we had a party there. Boys and girls, smokin joints, bottles of Vodka, music, all that. Mickey was meetin Susan's mate Patricia and they were goin off in the bedroom. Susan came over and sat beside me, I was only 15 at the time, she was 16. We were chattin away and she just started kissin me and put her hand down the front of me tracksuit bottoms and start pullin the balls of me.

Do yuh want to go in the room, she said
All I could do was say Yeah.

We went into Danny's Ma's bedroom and locked the door behind us. The blowjob she gave me is still one of the best I ever had. She taught me a few things that night and for the next two months, before I dumped her. She was a good ride but very annoyin, possessive, I couldn't look at another bird or she would go nuts. I wouldn't mind a blowjob off her now, I tell yuh.

Sellin drugs was the easiest way to make money when I was younger. Budgie and Rayo and me used to sell weed and then gear for Johnzer, and Johnzer was gettin off Tony scuzzball Horan, we were just small time, the bottom of the pile. Standin in the block, dealin. At 16, 17, makin 200 pound a day felt great. The blokes like Tony Scuzz we were gettin it off they were makin 5 grand a day and up the ladder the money gets better.

Us fools takin the risks on the street. The higher ups, most of them were pricks, lived in nice houses, big cars, wives, kids. Hadn't done any dirty work in years.

I was 14 years old when I had me first drug experience. After the usual day of playin football, games of heads and volleys in the block, gettin up to mischief.

David Molly and me were just standin around the back of the pram shed smokin a cigarette, puffin and passin it to each other, thinkin we were hardshots, it was one of them October days in Dublin, where everythin seems grey, like the concrete of the blocks of flats, grey sky, grey old faces of men lookin out over balconies smokin roll ups, dirty street pigeons grey, grey thoughts in yer head, as yuh see a single mother on the dole as she pushes her new born in the buggy to the grey walled rent office of the council to make an agreement on the debt she owes.

After we finished the smoke, I was pissin against the wall of the pram shed, tryin to get me piss to reach the top of the wall. David took out this small white bottle of

Tipp-Ex and said Here, do yuh wanna sniff some of this with me, it's a deadly buzz?

What does it do to yuh when yuh sniff it?

I can't explain it, yuh just have to do it, know what I mean?

Fuck it go on then, not here tho, somewhere we won't get caught

I know that yuh sap, we'll go over the back of the wall down at Billy's shop, no one will find us there, come on said David.

We went down to the lane at the back of Billy's shop, climbed the wall and over the other side. It was always filthy there, black bags with rubbish, bottles and cans lyin around, dead flies, the smell awful, piss and shit, used condoms, and syringes, a child's torn knickers with blood stains on them.

David took out two plastic sandwich bags and poured some Tipp-Ex into them, said to me, Take the bag and put it to yer mouth like this and start hoofin it out of it, breathin in an out real fast and hard, like me, watch.

He started inhalin the fumes from the white liquid in the corner of the bag. So I copied him and did the same, feelin nervous but I couldn't back out or David would laugh and tell everyone I was a pussy. After hoofin the fumes for a bit me face felt like it was on fire, I was dizzy, everythin sounded louder and deeper, could only move real slow, I laughed me head off and so did David. I thought David looked weird, evil, where they horns on his head?

I hoofed some more, then more, I felt like I left me body, me eyes rolled back, I stumbled and fell over, dropped the bag, the Tipp-Ex spilled out on me chin and onto the manky ground. When I snapped out of it, David was there slappin me in the face.

Wake up, come on Tommo yer all right, hee, hee, hee, David laughed manically.
I stood up and looked at him and said
That was deadly, where can we get more?

I started doin that shit nearly every day for about six months, not just Tipp-Ex, glue and the butane gas for lighters. A little gang of us would do it around the back of the shop or in someone's gaff if their ma and da had gone out for the night. What made us stop was the first real tragedy that happened in me life. Shawn Connelly dropped dead on his own at the back of the shop. David and Budgie found him there, twelve years old, lyin with all the dirt, empty cans, used condoms and piss stains, blood comin out from his nose and mouth, the bottle of gas still in his small pale hand. That was enough to scare the shit out of the rest of us, except Budgie the mad fuck, he still did the shit on his own for another two years. He'd claim proudly that, He loved the buzz and would do it all his life, even when he grew up and had a wife and kids.

I think the shock of findin Shawn dead like that really had an effect on Budgie, as yuh would expect. But there was no counsellin offered back then, yuh got on with it, It will make a man out of him da said. Well it didn't it made a mad bastard out of him, added to the fucked up shit he already had to deal with, livin in the flats, growin up like we did, he'd two older brothers who were real bullies and his ma and da were alcoholics, he never had much of a chance of growin up to be a man, another poor fucker, no wonder he ended up on the gear, dead from AIDS at twenty three, not a penny to his name, in fact he owed about two grand out, Johnzer paid for the funeral, God Bless yuh Budgie.

I remember Mountjoy prison and how it would go: rise at 7.30, a piss, maybe a shit as well in the toilet in the corner of me cell, wash, make the bed, have a smoke, do 50 sit ups, go down for breakfast, usually cereal, brin it back to the cell and eat it, a cup of tea to go with it and a smoke. The first cup of tea and a smoke are the best ones of the day. Do a bit of work, cleanin the landin, moppin floors, go the gym, do some weights, go to a class on computers, the yard, dinner, not much else, back in the cell for the night, maybe do some readin, and lights out, in bed asleep by 9.30-10.00. Most of the time in prison it's borin and that's what can really get to yuh. It's broke by violence, a scrap in the yard or someone gets stabbed or like that time a bloke called Steve Clarke came in, new to the landin. Word gets around like a forest fire that Stevo ripped off about twenty people on the wing for chicken soup passed off as gear. So out in the yard Stevo yappin away to Billy Green, talkin real loud, about how he's some sort of hard man. A gang of about 15 blokes, some who he ripped off, some just joinin in for the fun of it, swoop in real fast and attack, layin into him with fist and boots, it's fast and ferocious, like one of those BBC documentary's on loins and wildebeests. One fella takes out a shiv and cuts Stevo up bad, slash's his face and jabs him in the arms, shoulder, and chest a few times. He's left there shakin and in a pool of his own blood, cryin, the shiv beside him when the screws come and get him and it break up.

Someone shouts over

Cut himself shavin did he?

That's a bad nic he has there.

The pack laughs.

I felt no sympathy for him. We live by rules, street rules and a lot of people in the jail would go along with me, yuh don't rip people off for drugs, especially people from the areas that most of the people in there are from. Never rat to the Garda or screws. Stevo broke the rules and he got punished for it. Just like we broke society's rules and got punished and put in jail, that's how it is, don't cry or whinge about it.

Smelly, damp, cramped little cell. Ugly muck savage screws, lookin at yuh as if yuh were a bit of shit on their shiny fuckin shoes. Fuckin Muppets all over the wing. Talkin all the time about, I'm gonna kill 'em when I get 'em, this jump over they did, the chase they got from the Garda, most of this is all bullshit of course. Drugs everywhere. Cunts bangin up in the cells, sharin dirty needles. Fuckin Aids and Hep C infected bastards. Tablets, hash, coke everything's here. This one bloke, he's sharin a cell with another bloke, one of his best mates. Knew him his whole life. Yer man OD's. Dies in the bed, and yuh know what he done, his so called mate?

Searched his pockets and his person for heroin, yeah, he stuck his finger up his dead mates arse to see if he had any drugs up there. He's not gonna need them is he, he's fuckin dead, isin he, no point lettin it go to waste, is there? Yer man said to us. The dirt bag!

Walkin around the last remains of the block, the other day, it's gettin torn down and rebuilt. I sat on the small wall that went around what used to be playground, had another smoke, on the ground right under me feet I seen it,
Tommo loves Janice scratched in the cement. when we only started goin out with each other. Janice...
Janice was me girlfriend for two years.
We met when we were seventeen, her mate Linda came over and said
Here, she's mad about yuh, will yuh go out with her?

I looked over and saw this beautiful youngone there, blonde, great figure, nice blue eyes.
Tell her to come over and we can have a chat, he said.
She came over and we just hit it off.

The first time I took Ecstasy was one of the best nights I ever had. At a party in Janice's cousin Lisa's gaff in Finglas. There was loads of people there, Janice, Budgie, fatso, Simon, Mandy Kane, A few more from the flats, we all went out, Lisa's ninetieth birthday it was. This bloke called Savo took out a bag of yokes, there was 200 Speckled doves. 15 quid each unless yuh buy a few of them. Everyone swallows one each. Sittin there on the sofas, music's playin, people wafflin to each other, some

people dancin, blokes with their tops off. Half an hour
goes by and then the pills start comin up on us. Rubbin
hands together, rubbin heads, chewin lips, tappin feet,
talkin fast, gettin real deep in conversation, everyone's
huggin, tellin each other
I swear I love yuh man.
You're deadly.
See him, he's the best mate in the world he is.

Rushes of adrenaline and euphoria. Next of all tops were
off, Budgie, Rayo, me and all the lads in the gaff.
Dancin, just givin it socks, wreckin it as they would say.
Music gets into yuh and yuh get into the tune like never
before, and when yuh hear the tunes again when you're
sober, yuh get little flash backs, tingles, and yuh want to
get yokes that night, the tune it stays with yuh. Janice
looked more than sexy to me, fuckin mad shit like that
happens to yuh on them yokes.

I remember that time when we smuggled in a load of E's
into Mountjoy and it was Christmas got the whole wing
mad out of it of it the screws were drunk an all, The
whole of C-wing havin a big party with radio's and
bottles a whiskey and vodka, everyone on a mad love
buzz, it was, for once, worthy of the name The Joy.

I remember Janice's face when she found out I fucked
her best friend Tammy, or when she seen Louise Tierney
gettin out of me car fixin her skirt and hair, or the last
time when she picked up me phone and heard another
bird's voice say howya babe… Her face as she looked so

happy the day she married yerman Luke Benson from England, an Army fella, fuckin dopes the pair of them…

The first time I did gear, I smoked it. After one of them long two day and nights coke parties, the comedown is a cunt. Starin at the fuckin walls, sittin in a chair awake, but yer body drained. A few of us were there in the gaff, smokin joints, and stuck to the chairs, not sayin much, when Davo Martin, took out a quarter bag of heroin and asked if anyone minded if he smoked a few lines it's great for the come down. Work away we says, and then he says, dya any of yiz wanna smoke a bit, do yuh the world a good for the head, tellin yiz. Fuck it I says, once won't kill me, and bang, doin it ever since. Yuh know the story, big cliché, but true, do it on the weekends for the comedown, then its fuck it Wednesday night bored, telly is shit, might as well smoke a bit, then its Monday, and then its fuck the coke, I need a bag a gear, then the smokes not enough and yuh start bangin it up, and then yer proper fucked… like me…

The more the gear took over, everythin else went to shit, and I mean everythin! I sold everythin I owned and didn't own. A bare flat, with a bed, a table and a chair, few clothes that's it. Eventually the gaff is gone too, can't pay the rent, end up in jail, come out, back on the streets, and the hostels.

Yeah I know, I can hear yuh sayin that it's me own fault, alright, but here, are yuh a saint, yuh never got locked or stoned, or done somethings yuh shouldn't have? I heard a fella say once, that addiction is like a virus, if you're exposed to it yuh catch it, like the place yuh grow up, or the people around yuh, everyone's doin it, the place is fuckin flooded with it, not everyone there catches it, but even if they don't, someone close to them does, a brother, a cousin, a best mate.

Last time in the Joy I did six months for a loada shity little charges. Somethin changed tho, I just had enough, finally had enough. I got on the drug free unit, and got clean, I'm doin well, clean a year now, still out on the streets tho, I have a tent for meself, and sometimes make the hostels. If I could just get a chance, a small gaff, an address, I'd be grand, I could have that little somethin of me own again. Please god I get through this next winter. Thanks for listenin. Cya around.
Hopefully.
God Bless.

What The Minister for Housing Proposes: Thinking Outside The Council House
by
Kevin Higgins

Easy for the Opposition
to hang around overheated TV studios,
spouting impossible promises
which at this stage sound
like a recorded message from Santa Claus.
But out there, in what I like to call
the world, a constituent of mine
and his wheelchair recently spent
the coldest night of the year
in a discontinued telephone box
and, worse than that, there are people
who have nothing better to do
than use this situation as an excuse
to be atrocious to Government Ministers
on Twitter.

If we as a country,
who, relatively speaking, lived mainly
in tumbled-in cottages
and could barely afford trousers
until around about last Friday,
are to get past this glitch
we need to start thinking
outside the traditional council house –
which, like communism,
selling encyclopaedias door to door,
and National Health glasses,

isn't coming back.

First thing tomorrow morning
immediately after my Eggs Benedict
I will introduce tax breaks incentivising
those that have them to rent out every available
wardrobe and wheelie bin
to those who through some bad life
decision have found themselves caught
between tiny thousand quid a month flats.

Given the lack of such facilities
in your average wheelie bin or wardrobe,
every qualifying adult will be issued with a potty
which may be emptied anywhere except
over the Minister for Housing's head.

And under subsection seven
of my Housing Emergency Provisions act
infants inconsiderate enough to have been born
without fixed abode will be confined
to newly tax deductible sideboard drawers
so they won't grow up
to take more space
than the world has for them.

Land[*]
by
Viviana Fiorentino

I kiss you

between my tongue

and   your
tongue
(I look for a place   /the
exact space)

I bury the scents of memories
(a new tongue cannot tell what we've been through).

This is the land, a pause of time,

this is the land I looked
for.

This is the land, the gesture of your fingers,

when you open your palm
as a rose.

This is the land, the place where we wait for
a ray of light –
it won't leave our bones.

Life stripped our clothes.

Naked, a ground still has flesh below.

[*] published in: Honest Ulsterman issue February 2021; in Mantis magazine, Stanford University, issue 16 (2021)

Between land and sea^(*)
by
Viviana Fiorentino

The harbour, a safe passage from sea to land

Night
iron oxide stains
dark
cadmium sulphide,
mercury,
and the colour of the sky
colour Cassel Earth
deep peat,
crumbled.

Migrating underground.

The eyes know petrels, above
they fly miles over sky paths.

Here we are blind
(yet we know the way).

Here we breathe through the skin
(yet we hold hope).

Divided between two continents, we name the sea
distance
(because the body remembers each breakage in the
bones).

Migrating underground.

While the night is a road

pointing towards what we desire

we rise from
under water, underground,

in a skin tight envelop

we emerge

to be free and imagine

       miles above our heads   yet swans and petrels
                                        are flying.

(*) 10.6.18, the Italian Home Office Minister prevented
the Aquarius, capacity 500, from docking. 630 migrants,
including more than 100 children and people tortured in
North Africa, were on board.

Shoreline I
by
Viviana Fiorentino

On the shore, our feet close.

We float.

No reasons to see sky-ward.

We are now made of this.

The horizon swallows sea shore rocks.

We don't arrive
 we stay, in a mist beyond islands - off they ride on seas.

We don't leave
                we stay, in cold salty weeds and grief - the
                sea eroding lands and lands under our feet.

Years fading.
Seasons of the soul.

Home Sweet Home
by
Anne Tannam

i

Little pig, little pig, let me come in.
No, no, not by the hair on my chinny chin chin.
Then I'll huff, and I'll puff, and I'll blow your house in.

ii

At night when IKEA shoppers leave,
their trolleys piled high with picture frames,
picnic essentials for al fresco dining, cushions,
bedding, scented candles, bathroom accessories,

a trolley is dragged backwards up the escalator,
reversing along the designated pathway,
a hand returning, item after item to their places,
slowly emptying the trolley of its contents.

iii

We avoid passing our old house on our way to school,
though it means an extra twenty minutes walking;
on wet days the kids get drenched and there's
nowhere to hang wet clothes in the B&B.

iv

Jack has the dream again: he's standing in the lane
behind their old house,
face pressed against the garden door. There's Darren
from his old school
splashing in the paddling pool that Ma threw out years
ago,

splashing and laughing like it's his back garden, his toys
on the grass,
his treehouse, and Jack shouts at him, *Leave my fucking
toys alone,*
but Darren doesn't turn round, can't hear Jack's muffled
words screamed into the pillow.

v
Have you no home to go to?
vi
And I am praying to God on high,
And I am praying Him night and day,
For a little house - a house of my own,
Out of the wind's and the rain's way.

(A version of this poem first appeared in the North, Issue
61, guest edited by Nessa O'Mahony and Jane Clarke.)

Raftery in the Night
by
Eamon Mag Uidhir

The coldness has come on me and
       there is silence throughout this
strange house, excepting the crack of a
       contemptuous log ember and an
insidious draught whistling yonder where
       there should be a proper curtain.

They've left me alone—as they all do
       once they've gorged their sentimental
appetites, scraping vicarious lamentation
       from my verse as I scrape poignant
notes of pain and dispossession from
       my battered fiddle—left me alone in
this dwindling fireplace glow with only
       an old dog nuzzling my knee for
friend or company and a rag of a
       blanket a beggar wouldn't spit
on cast around my shoulders.

Tomorrow the frosty road, and if I'm
       fortunate a seat on the back of a
cart, and if I'm luckier still with a
       half-crown in my breeches instead
of a paltry shilling—if my upstart
       lord of tonight and his port-swilling
lady have felt their wild romantic livers
       shiver at my songful words of death
and the drowning of poor folk.

From Red Biddy
by
Fran Lock

red biddy

noun

a mixture of cheap wine and methylated spirits.

biddy

noun

of unknown origin; probably influenced by the use of *biddy* denoting an Irish maidservant, from *Biddy*, pet form of the given name *Bridget.*

'All you young people now take my advice
Before crossing the ocean you'd better think twice'
– Jimmy MacCarthy

1

ever hear the one about the man with two shadows?

one was a matador's cape, the other a thin girl cut from the queasy cloth of her own bad self. this is a Monday, mind. fire weaving hawkweed into hacking cough. he slipped his plimsolls running. leapt the fence. spread his hand to find his cocksure fortune full of thorns. took his torn palm into town, tarried his swaggering luck through lanes. bantam boy, bantering, jaw-jacked scally in the jackdaw dawn. his aggie ma, hauling his name across coals all the days of her life, till it rose on the roof of her mouth like a blister. scar of his slingshot pedigree. he'd never come back, each delinquent sinew stretched its short electric measure. said his going *ripped the lining* from her eyes. if sons were *sovvies*, silvered in the silk-purse of her seeing. said she wore his beaming counterfeit smooth across one side. and oh, he was the ether's genii then, dreamt his chequered pleasures, walked each night towards the guillotine of sleep with baby steps. he was *away*, trailing his lustrous brawn through forecourts, car parks, foreclosed farms. following the bitter ribbon of the road to the north, to the west, to the ford-mouth of the hostings, to the old men buckled by husbandry, gingham girls in the grip of small town non-event. and oh, that canny lad, that diamond bruiser, that one time baron of Ballinasloe –

and this was the man with two shadows? tell me.

i was coming to that. always i was coming. how he slept under hedges. his shadow was his pillow and his bindle and he carried the whole world knotted up in one wet corner of it. how he was spring's pilgrim, hobnail apostle of the copse and culvert, anything cooked in a smoky hole. and it was thin going, till the whole dark sea laid out before him like a lead apron. and he paid his passage in *coarse words for common objects,* and his passage was long, and he slept standing up like a horse. how sometimes you're not even moving, how a hard road travels the length of a man, his romanestan swelling and stretching inside. and he slept on the docks in his shadow, bound in its red-green wastrel cloak. and blue. when a man's hand is his flag, and you can read his shadow like the grimoire of his poxy fate, and his

mother's voice in an auger shell, on and on, remorseless
and rokkering. god. in Liverpool they tell him his gold
tooth's got by alchemy, and they try his gilded tongue
for passing twice through a wishing ring, and they
sharpen their telepathy on the edge of a desk, and cut
down the tree on which his mother carved his birth, and
his mother's voice ran silent then, as a stream runs mud.

is all this true?

yes. and his first shadow was a sling, and he carried his
arms and his hunger in it. and his own mother wouldn't
know him from a scarecrow. and they called him *scrub
tinker*, not even fit for sorting scrap. and he chewed all
night on his daddy's blackberry blood, mulled her pale
face too, poor cow, who bore her grief like a basket of
knives and could not love him. he could not sit still. he
would not be the work of many hands. chased from
verges, grim billets of wasteland. wanted away and he
ran. but that tongue, lord, inching through the soily
hours of darkness like a worm, has its own earth-
cravings, must speak brick-dust dirt to loam, or find a
way to sing.

and of the other shadow?

saw *her* by the union chapel, Hawley road, driving
spears of heather through the plush lapels of enemy
gents like she wanted them staked and dead. they were
frisking her lingo for a telltale cluck when she spat in
their faces: *talk to me about* resilience, *I'll grind your
bones to make my bread.* pikey. worse. poshrat, answers

to the suck of air between a plumber's teeth. and has no name. cuts her hair to a cold hearth breathing soot, and doesn't care. she has no tongue, she does not eat. nurses pry her teeth apart. all they find inside is another man's fist.

this shadow is dangerous.

yes. but how like himself. and takes his hand. flailing his work-shy meat in a warehouse. body, a deviant dance against gravity. hard life. lucks into sudden colour when she is near. a gallon jug of thunderbird, a tin of tea. an ambulance racing somebody to somewhere in the painterly night. mad Alan with his rat tattoo, gone off his trolley in a squat. the waify and immaterial few, whose high a rome where all these mainline mazes lead. these lesser roads. these vandals and these goths. London is a cloned ghost mouthing her sweet nothings in every window. is a window for every ghost. the squat, that squat, that garrison of discontent. the rec ground gone to nettles, sad behind Paddington, sweating out its lairy yellow threat, its green seam split, its ambush of weeds. affrighted edge, the paring blade of *any*where. London tests her raging mettle, his. lies with his back pushed into the earth, holding the whole world up by its ripped mattress. becomes a bootleg Christ, sprawled and gormless against the plank he'll walk to crucifixion. oh, *she* says there's beauty in a daggered light like strangulation. folds him, strokes the clammy threads of his disorder smooth. bathes him in another name. not the moniker that swaddled him, but something rushy, wet. fixes his blood to hers with a razor's partial grace. her fingers falter holes in his lobes with a pin till he's pricked all over like a grubby bud of lace.

but how did they become tied?

i was coming to that. always i was coming. all her life, she said, she was smeared across the threshold of some man, worn in his buttonhole, drowned in his poacher's pocket. and she ran too. made herself anew from a ragbag of silky fixings. scraped herself from barrel bottoms, sucked the pennies out of fountains clean. read borrow. said *he's well named* and vexed his mildew-muddled ghost in stoppered bottles. read the world with gleaning eye, said *oh, i rue the day i dipped my biddy tongue in your foul cant.* England, where the torchlight traipses over her. where her pavee ariettas are the meat the organ grinds to tuneful mince. and spoilt. she wanted the world. not to treasure, but to smash. to master its daggers and turn them back on the hands that held them, to drag their bleeding précis' through her patois' gutter gorse, each faltering declension a barb in their softly moral hide. he was too hurt. wanted the voodoo of spoons, the sweet numb sleep, and a lasting drink of red. his vision drizzled into constellation. they have *no word for stars*, borrow said. oh, but please, a fulsome argot of moons. she tied him with her own cut hair. with Shrove candles, baked apples, their subtle fragrance sealed in heat, her own wrists swimming in beeswax and blood, the golden sear on greyish meat, the burning of bundles of sage. flimsy bonds. shapeless kite, mithered by wind. barely snagged at her ravelled edge.

so they became torn?

in secret he'd fed his first shadow. it grew so big, shaking its rusty antlers. wran jag mask, dancer at the wake. shadow number one now a furbearing fluke of pain with his mother's face. in his dreams the camp and the last of the fire, eating through sleep's thin celluloid strips. and London's vicious bridges, bearing his weary guilt on their backs. *coward*, they called him, *cunning.* work was long when work was to be had. and morning's fearsome cold enough to drive the tattoos from his skin. he had no words, but those words going forth by day on the book of himself. how rocks tear the underbellies of boats, a thought of home would surprise him. where *home* is not a shore but a tongue that begs to wag. ganger, gavver, gaffer, they flattened him to *paddy,* poor *paddy,* a word with a chaser of bile brought forth from your own loathe gut. the north and its blethering fevers. a stubby finger stabbing his chest at closing time: *which side are you on?* until *home* is a chandelier sinking to the bottom of a wreck, is a dropped needle scoring a song through dusty shellac.

and so?

he ran. at first she clung to his back like a hump of his own dull flesh, but he slipped her when she was stringing her words into makeshift bandoliers some throbbing morning. how the last thing she said with a look like getting straight was *i don't know how to help you.* and he was going back. and she was eating the night

into abstinence. her tongue could cut water. his formed a
wick trimmed especial for poison tallow.

and so?

he drank. he died.

and so?

you know. that look on her face, that body all lithe and
pious, poised when you ask her where she's from to rip
your fucking throat out. you know full well. when she
sits still and throws a sundial's shape across paper. yes.
did you hear the one, did you hear the one now, did you
hear the one about the woman with two shadows?

Everything
by
Glenn Gannon

Tired of being cooped up in the house,.. we went for a walk in the rain,..the streets were deserted and the golden harvest moon was on the wane,..there was still some cars but mostly they were headed out of town,..trying to beat the midnight deadline,.. for another Covid lockdown,

I told my wife I was sorry,.. I let the kids put her in that home,..I thought that it was for the best at the time,.. I didn't know that she would pass away all alone,..my mind is in utter confusion almost every day,..I can't believe that after fifty years My darling is gone away,..I turned around and headed back home, the rain was getting heavier you see, and in the window of a shop I saw a lonely old man,.. alone and staring back at me,.. I put the key into my front door and hung my overcoat in the hall,..then I made a cup of tea as the clock ticked loudly on the wall,.. I picked up our photo from the mantel,.. It was the day that we were Wed,.. the clock cant tick fast enough for me now,.. I don't want to live without her,.. my heart is broken and I'd much rather be dead,.. I hope that God will forgive me,.. for saying such a terrible thing,..the pain of loss is much too great to bear,.. when you have lost your everything.

The Astral Pilgrim
by
Glenn Gannon

My mind is an astral pilgrim, it goes where ever it will,.. sometimes atop a mountain or to a cabin on a hill,.. it traverses continents like an eagle gliding on a thermal breeze,.. it soars up high and swoops down low with efficiency and ease,.. I acquired this skill as a boy of seven years,.. it was my portal of escape for me and an end to all my fears, mankind is rooted to earthly things bound tight by wealth's glittering allure,.. I care not for material things they are not mankind's cure,.. if money be the root of all evil,.. then spending one's life in search of it is madness to be sure,.. therefore use your wealth to help those who are in need,.. those who have nothing at all,.. and you will store up graces in Heaven,.. for when you hear the good Lords heavenward call.

A Mother And Her Child
At Christmas In The 1950s
by
Glenn Gannon

When I was just five Christmas's old,.. My Mam
brought me by the hand through the snow we went,.. it
was so very cold,.. my breath made little steam clouds
that floated on the icy air,.. I watched them go and as I
did so snowflakes alighted upon my hair,.. what was this
Magic that was all around,.. bright coloured lights,..
sparkling frost atop the snow on the ground,.. glistening
glittering like the Christmas Tree where Santa knelt
down to talk to me,.. I nodded my head as I peeked out
from behind my Mam,.. "be a good little boy" Santa said,
or I'll only bring you, a slice of bread and jam,.. My
Mam picked me up and kissed me, I could smell her
comforting perfume,.. we waved bye bye to Santa who
gave me a blue wrapped gift, as we left his little room,..
on the way down town,.. through a sea of bustling
people I looked up at the dark sky to the tip of St
Patrick's Steeple,.. the stars were twinkling like the
crusty ice that layered the snow before us,.. the bus stops
were packed along by the Coombe and somewhere a
choir sang Silent Night as Mam and I sang the chorus,
Later that night as Mam tucked me into my cosy bed,..
she gently brushed the hair from my face, kissed my
rosy cheeks,.. and I love you was all she said.

'They paid dearly for their devotion to the national cause'

by
Liz Gillis

The story of women and the part they played in the fight for Irish freedom thankfully has been brought to the fore. Over the last twenty years, new records have been released; documents long hidden in attics have been rediscovered. And they are telling the stories of those who were not the 'big names' of the Irish Revolution and who without their involvement, there would not have been an independence movement. But there is still so much to discover about this period of our history. The War of Independence 1919-1921 was a time of fear and terror in Ireland. Yet thousands of men and women risked everything for the freedom of their country.

The activities of Cumann na mBan, the women's revolutionary movement are well documented. They were dispatch carriers, nursed wounded IRA men, gathered intelligence, kept safe houses and much, much more. But what price did they pay for their activities? The women were on the frontline. The home became a battleground – their home, a place where they should have felt safe, was not. And while very few women were killed in the conflict, compared to IRA or military, a way to cause great harm was to target their homes.

I would like to share with you the stories of four formidable women, who risked everything and lost practically everything because of their involvement in the fight for Irish freedom.

Máire Murphy née Cuffe was from Cromogue, Ferns in County Wexford. Together with her sister Peg, they set up an Irish speaking school in their home at Cromogue in 1917. The school was very successful; it had 20 students including some borders. Yet their home was not just a centre of education, it was also a centre of IRA activity.

In 1920 Máire joined Cumann na mBan and became Captain of the Kilmyshal/Cromogue Branch. While she and Peg were teaching, they were also sheltering IRA men who were on the run from the authorities. They hid guns and ammunition, nursed sick and wounded Volunteers and pretty soon they came to the attention of the authorities. In February 1921, at the height of the War of Independence, their home was burned down by the Black and Tans. They lost everything, 'not a stone upon stone of the house or school was left'. They had nowhere to go and were forced to sleep in a barn. As a result, Máire's health suffered, she had a nervous breakdown but she did not give up. The sisters continued to teach in a stable and fowl house that had escaped the fire as well as their revolutionary activities. And they rebuilt their home and school.

Bella Lucas was from Derrycastle, Ballina, County Tipperary and joined Cumann na mBan in 1918. She was a member of the 3rd Battalion Branch, Tipperary No. 1 Brigade. One of the vital roles undertaken by the women was that of Intelligence. The authorities were slow to realise just how involved the women were and Bella Lucas is a prime example of this.

Her aunt, Ida Molony owned a pub on Bridge Street, Killaloe, County Clare which was a favourite haunt of the Auxiliaries. The 'Auxies', as they were called, had a fearsome reputation and left behind a trail of destruction wherever they went. However, one Auxie was fond of Ida and talked and talked, giving information on planned raids etc. Ida in turn passed on this information to Bella who would inform the local IRA officers. But her luck ran out, the Auxies knew she was involved and were determined to make her pay. Her home was regularly raided. One can only imagine how terrifying it would be as these raids generally happened at night.

On one occasion Bella recalled, 'they took me out in the night and threatened to shoot me if I did didn't tell them where I was getting my information'. She didn't tell. They didn't stop there, they came back and on the 27 June 1921, Bella's home was burned down. Like Máire Murphy and the countless others this had happened to, Bella had nowhere to go and had to sleep in an outhouse, this in turn affected her health. She had a nervous breakdown, followed by Rheumatic Fever and she never fully recovered. Despite the fact that she had lost her home and her health was broken, she still continued working with the IRA.

Sara McDonnell was from Pallas, Cahir, County Tipperary and came from a Republican family. Her four brothers were members of the IRA and she and her sister were members of Youghalarra Branch, Cumann na mBan. On one occasion the police raided her home and a gun was found. Her father and brother were arrested. The McDonnell home was well and truly on the radar of the police and military after that. Yet their home was always open to the IRA. IT became the headquarters for the 3rd Battalion, North Tipperary Brigade and Sara was always on hand to assist. She cooked for the IRA, scouted for them, brought dispatches to different units and looked after guns and ammunition. But the authorities were never far away.

In April 1921, while conduction a raid at the family home, the Auxies fired at Sara and her cousin while they were in their yard. A month later they returned and this time they were going to send a very clear message. On 27 April 1921, the IRA attacked the police barracks in Portroe. The McDonnell home was chosen as the target for an official reprisal and on 1 May the Crown Forces destroyed the house. The family were forced to camp on the land for three months. Yet it wasn't enough for the authorities. Sara got word that they were going to come back one night and completely destroy their camp and they were forced to go on the run. Due to the hardship she suffered, Sara became very ill and ended up in hospital. Yet when she recovered, she was back with the IRA, carrying on as before.

Whereas Sara McDonnell, Bella Lucas and Máire Murphy were members of Cumann na mBan, there were a number of women who were deliberately told *not* to join. They would have to be completely unknown to the authorities.

One such lady was Marian Tobin of Tincurry House, Cahir, County Tipperary. She was one of, if not the most trusted people in Tipperary and was held in such high regard by those members of the IRA who she worked with. Marian Tobin was a widow with a young family, but her home was always open to the 3rd Tipperary Brigade, IRA. Sean Treacy, Dan Breen, Seamus Robinson and Sean Hogan were frequent visitors. Not only did she feed and care for them, her home was used for Brigade meetings, she hid guns, drove the men around, carried dispatches. As she later recalled, 'During the entire period of the war I was on the alert and ready to harbour Commandant Robinson, Breen and Hogan'. Apart from her revolutionary activities, she also made history by being the first woman to be elected as a County Councillor in Tipperary in 1920.

Unable to prove her connection to the IRA, the authorities still had Marian in their sights and her home was raided numerous times, but nothing was ever found. But her luck also ran out. As an official reprisal for the killing of D.I. Potter by the IRA, hers was a number of houses targeted for destruction by the Crown Forces. On 14 May, 1921 they came. There was only Marian and her thirteen year old daughter Eva in Tincurry House at the time. They were only allowed to take some clothes. The police found nothing, despite searching everywhere. They gave no reason for the search. They smashed everything, nothing could be salvaged. And when they were done, they dealt the final blow and bombed the house. Tincurry House was a ruin. But Marian was defiant and continued her revolutionary activities.

So there are the stories of four women who were made homeless due to their activities during the War of Independence. They are the tip of the iceberg; their story is replicated in towns and villages across Ireland. But one thing shines through about these women and it can be said of the people of Ireland at the time – they were defiant. Their homes may have been destroyed and their future very bleak but they never gave up and they carried on with even more determination. The forces of the greatest empire the world have ever seen tried to destroy their spirit, they failed.

To The Arsehole who ruined my Favourite film:
by
Dylan Henvey

We had waited so long for the book launch.

The Virus, the lockdown, the elusive vaccine, it seemed that day would never come, or worse, it would be done over zoom. Just another event to add to the long list of what were Previously (open to argument) enjoyable experiences ruined by zoom – zoom chats, zoom catch ups, zoom coffee, Zoom Drinks, Zoom quizzes, zoom bingo, zoom karaoke for Christ sake. All of the aforementioned zooms carried varying degrees of cringe, and/or levels of awkwardness which usually culminated in me physically placing at least one hand over my mouth in a desperate attempt to prevent myself from screaming I DON'T CARE WHAT YOUR FUCKING BANANA BREAD TASTES LIKE! But a Zoom charity book launch would have really taken the biscuit, or really taken the Banana bread should I say.

Thankfully Mercy prevailed and as the room slowly filled in Pearse Street Library, I made a Bee line for the free wine. Small talk and Chit Chat have never been my strong points, a Glass or two of wine had always helped, if not for the intoxication, then merely to sip at between any awkward silences which were certain to occur. Tonight the Wine would be needed more than ever, several notable writers and authors had made contributions to the anthology. As I went for a refill of wine I skimmed a glance around the room in order to catch a glimpse of the Writers of note. Social awkwardness has gotten the better of me on more than one occasion, so to avoid it going forward I had developed the overtly mature approach, of guzzling glasses of wine and avoiding at all costs those most likely to activate any feelings of social inadequacy.

It was at this moment I first seen him, Standing in the top corner of the room. Just to the right of the stage. A strange man or, at least a man doing things that could be considered strange. He was standing half turned away from the rest of the crowd, with his head almost bowed, muttering words to himself, without break or pause of any kind. I turned my head to take stock of the remaining wine; I better go easy I thought, that poor fucker needs it more than me. He's probably too embarrassed to be seen helping himself to the wine I thought. Sure, I says to meself, I'll play the Good Samaritan, bring him over a glass. But Before I could take a step in his direction, he had begun to move toward the stage. He shuffled toward the podium and stood there, holding a glare to the humming crowd. In turn the Crowds attention gradually meandered toward the man on stage and a hush fell cautiously across the room. I reached slowly to my pocket like a cowboy to his holster, I drew my Phone. I don't know what it was, don't ask me to explain it, but Something told me there and then that whatever story this man had to tell I had to capture it.

Without leaving you in any further suspense let me show you the video;

(The man on stage Zips down a black hoody top to reveal an I HEART JESUS T-shirt and several reels of rosary beads round his neck. From his right hand pocket he drew a book and held it aloft (it appeared to be a bible)

My name is Richard Devine. For the last Forty days and forty nights UNDER COVER FOR THE LEGION OF MARY, I have worked in and lived over the SWEET SENSATIONS ADULT SEX TOY SUPERSTORE on St James Street.

(at this point I says to myself; I guess I was wrong, embarrassment clearly isn't something this fella suffers with)

And that's what has brought me here this evening - when I look out at this crowd I see some familiar faces, some very familiar faces indeed!

(This is gonna be good I thought to myself with a squirm of excitement, wouldn't say I'm the only one feeling the social anxiety anymore! Then Holy Joe on stage took a long pause and eyeballed the whole room almost one by one, I pan the camera toward the crowd, to see who's feeling the heat, to see if there's anyone twitching nervously in their seat or looking for the emergency exits, but no one flinched, great I thought, this is going to be some real life x-rated version of that board game guess who)

Jesus went out into the desert for forty days and forty nights in order to face Satan and all the temptation he had to offer. It was only after this could he begin his ministry in Galilee. Six months ago I was Baptised and born again, I accepted Jesus Christ our lord as my one true saviour and devoted my life to serving god. But just like Jesus, I too would have to face temptation before I began my ministry. So I set myself out into the desert, into the Barron wilderness of saint James Street, to face the Devil, and all the temptation he had to offer in SWEET SENSATIONS ADULT SEX TOY SUPERSTORE on St James Street.

And there the devil did tempt me, just as he tempted Jesus; through Lust of the Eyes and Lust of the Body and lust of the Soul. As some of you in the crowd well know – there is a small cinema located to the back of SWEET SENSATIONS ADULT SEX TOY SUPERSTORE on St James Street. Each day a visually impaired man named Stephen would visit the shop. Stevie wonder the Locals called him, after the famous blind musician. He would come straight after morning mass. I've just confessed my sins he would say, 'time to sin some more'. He would ask me to select an Adult DVD for him, to watch in the small cinema in the back. On the big screen he could just about make out the images. As some of you are well aware there is a huge collection of DVDs in the store. Stephen would stand there listening as I reeled off the movie titles. It was at this point I came to realise that these vile pornographic film makers took their villainy even further – they parodied their sordid films on famous Hollywood movies. Stephen would slap his white cane (pauses, and views the audience with disdain) HIS GUIDE STICK, at a particular DVD, like an old head master lashing his cane against the blackboard demanding an answer 'wha's tha one?'

"*Titty Titty bang bang*" (blesses himself, mutters forgive me lord)

Crack against the case 'wha's tha one?'

"*Forest Hump*" (blesses himself, mutters forgive me lord)

Crack against the case 'wha's tha one?'

Throbbin Hood and his many men (blesses himself, mutters forgive me lord)

Crack against the case 'wha's tha one?'

"*Edward Penis hands* "(blesses himself, mutters forgive me lord)

Crack against the case 'And tha won'

"*Sleeping booty*" (blesses himself, mutters forgive me lord)

'Tha one'?

"*Fill Bill*"

(This is like a feckin episode of little Britain he's describing)

Crack against the case 'wha's tha one?

"*In Diana Jones -raiders of the lost arse* "(blesses himself, mutters forgive me lord)

Crack against the case 'wha's tha one?'

"*Schindlers Fist* "((blesses himself three times, whimpers Oh Lord forgive me)

'Wha's tha one?'

FEW HARD MEN "

'Oh I've seen that one' said Stephen 'do you know what Ur man says ta Ur wan?'

And it was in that moment I seen it, the vulgar smile which Besmirched his face and lit up his grey eyes, was Beelzebub himself there tempting! Tempting my curiosity! I right there in SWEET SENSATIONS ADULT SEX TOY SUPERSTORE on St James Street. I closed my eyes and clenched my Jaw and prayed to Jesus for strength. Stephen continued; he says to her "you want the flute! You can't handle the flute! "But let me tell ya something 'she surly could handle the flute if ya know wha I mean 'ja know wha I mean eh? Ja know wha I mean eh?, Ja know wha I mean eh? Again and again the same words echoed in my ears, ja know wha I mean eh?' Then I heard another voice and it pleaded with me in a compassionate tone "just tell him you know what he means, I know you know what he means, you know you know what he means, just tell him you know' it was Satan himself!

I held tight for a couple more moments, waiting for Stephens's lewd laughter to fizzle out. Then I heard a loud bang and I opened my eyes Stephen was nowhere to be seen, he had disappeared, I had won. I had stared down sin and vanquished the devils first temptation! Well, when I say he had disappeared he had actually tripped over a box prosthetic Vaginas which I had left in the middle of the floor. He wasn't hurt or anything so it was fine. I took this as holy Imagery – The Sinner had been floored if not entirely vanquished, a sign from god. I was on the right Path. I did however cancel my Netflix subscription that same evening – after that day much of the movie content had been tainted forever.

That night Lucifer came to me in a Lucid Dream with his next temptation- Lust of the body. He offered to make me an adult movie star. Instead of Richard Devine my performance name would be Dick Devine….I would only ever have to make one movie he said. In that one Movie every Thrill, every titillation, every fantasy, every arousal, my every desire would be satisfied. The movie would be the highest grossing adult film of all time. I would be a millionaire. Every material desire met for as long as I shall live. He held out a contract for me to sign. I was so very tempted. The devil handed me a Pen, a golden, Twenty four carat, Diamond encrusted pen. I held the tip of the pen to the contract to sign. I paused. 'What's troubling you asked the Devil, what more could a man want or need? Oh I know. Of course, don't worry; we'll stick a couple of Inches on the end of your lad as well. For good measure wha! All you have to do is sign here.......oh, and ya can keep the pen.'

I looked down at the contract. My hand trembled; oh I wanted to sign, how I wanted to sign. Then I see the title of the film, Dick divine stars in legion of Mary's.

Legion of Marys! I was horrified. No, no I don't want this; I don't want any of this. I only need one Mary, and I do not mean that sort of Mary, I mean Mother Mary, holy Mary Mother of God. Now go, go get out! I woke suddenly in my bed, in the Grimy one room bedsit over SWEET SENSATIONS ADULT SEX TOY SUPER STORE on St. James Street. My heart racing, my sheets soiled. But I had resisted the devil Again.

The following week I was clearing out the store room. I began to come across some very peculiar items, even by the crude standards of SWEET SENSATION ADULT SEX TOY SUPERSTORE on St James Street; these items were strange - Edible body custard and Jelly Lube. WHAT are you to make some sort of fucking trifle I thought? What are these I asked the owner? 'Oh them, they're spire shaped dildos. I got the idea from Effie tower ones I seen online, which are very popular. I thought they'd be a seller with the tourists, but too narrow at the top apparently....you can have one if ya want'. Then I opened another box. I was instantly filled with utter detest, for the owner, for myself, for the human race, somehow how I managed to find the courage to ask 'Why have we got these? 'Oh those are the crucifixion Dildos, now those were a big seller during the pope's visit back in 2018, along with the naughty Nun outfits and Pervy priest costumes. That Pope's visit was great couple o' days for business that's for sure'. I was horrified. I could feel my soul ache. I wanted to run away. I knew it was Satan testing me, testing my will, testing my soul, 'Nothing compared to the 1916 stuff of course' the owner continued. 'There should be a few of "The Rising" penis pumps laying around in a box in here somewhere'. Romantic Irelands Dead and gone I thought to myself. 'The Michael Collins sex dolls are all gone o' course, had to order them in special, had to be custom made, very expensive. Supply and demand yano, as long as there is a demand I'll keep supplying' said the owner. He was right. It wasn't the shop. It wasn't the Items in it, it was the people. Nothing was sacred anymore. I ask you that, you being patrons of SWEET SENSATIONS ADULT SEX TOY SUPERSTORE on St James Street. Is anything scared anymore? Spiritually or culturally is anything sacred. The sinners multiply and the innocent divide. How could I ever make a difference in this wicked world? It was then at my darkest hour as I felt my faith beginning to wane the Virgin Mary appeared to me in the corner of the store room of SWEET SENSATIONS ADULT SEX TOY SUPERSTORE on St James Street. Her face appeared to me on a blow up inflatable doll. She spoke to me and said 'Remember the word of God and Remember the word of God is in you' then with a gentle gush of air the doll deflated in front of me. The buzzer sounded at the shop door. I rushed to answer it. In came a couple of regulars. They came in every week, after they had finished in their writing group in the city. I see you here tonight, do not worry I will not name your names.

(fucking spoil sport or wha!!)

The owner asked them what he could do for them.

'I'm here to collect a package' one of them replied

What is it called? Asked the owner

'ROSEBUD" replied one of the writers.

Rosebud. I knew that reference once. It was from a movie called Citizen Kane. My mother's favourite film.

We watched the old Black n white pictures together when I was a child.

We would watch Citizen Kane and she would tell me "You are my Rosebud, You are my rosebud do you know that, you are the only happiness I have ever known, in my entire life you are the only one that's made me happy"

You see my mother had not had an easy life. Her mother had died during child birth and her father had gone to Prison when she was Six. She never told me why, in fact she never spoke of him at all. She was sent to live in various homes and with various foster families. It hadn't been a happy time. She had suffered a lot as a child I was sure of that. She never spoke about it. But I knew she had by how often she cried. She died of a heroin overdose when I was 9 years old. I had never forgotten the old black and white pictures we watched together.

I felt this was a sign, a sign from heaven, a sign from her. Then it struck me, Citizen Kane was a retelling of the teaching of a book from the bible Ecclesiastes A man who had experienced everything and done everything, but in the end nothing is ultimately reliable. Death levels all. The only good is to partake of life in the present, for enjoyment is from the hand of God. . The world is filled with injustice. People should enjoy, but should not be greedy; no-one knows what is good for humanity; righteousness and wisdom escape us. All people face death, but we should enjoy life when we can. Mortals should take pleasure when they can, for a time may come when no one can.

Now I seen how cunning Satan had been, he had been tempting my soul all along, tempting me to hate the Sinner rather than the sin. Wanting me to forget the most important message in the Bible "love thy neighbour." If I truly wanted to help people I had to learn to be more open, more accepting, less judgemental. If what made people happy was covering themselves in edible body custard and watching" Titty Tittty bang bang" then that was between them and god.

From that day forward I decided I would help god by loving thy neighbour so they would not end up alone and neglected like my mother all those year ago.

That evening in My Grimy one room bed sit over SWEET SENSATIONS ADULT SEX TOY SUPERSTORE on St James Street. I decided to watch Citizen Kane. I had renewed my Netflix subscription. Before I turned on the film I googled the Item the Writers had come to collect from the store. What was Rosebud? I typed it in and I was speechless. 'Give that Fuck tunnel more Pucker than ever before. Inflate your asshole into a bulging rosebud with the rosebud anal pump' as I read the words a triumphant sneer erupted, and thundered around the room. It was like Jet engines taking off in each ear. Satan was having the last laugh. I did not watch the film. I cancelled my Netflix subscription again. But I came here tonight to say to you in the crowd. To the arsehole who ruined my favourite film – I forgive you.

Dedicated to Nicky Earley

What You Keep
by
Cheryl Vail

the attic fan's helicopter-rumble soundtracked July-1995
the exhausted air conditioner   declining to join the disharmony   that meant nothing
to a teenager minus a month   except   sheets clinging to humid skin

every morning a meditation   don't get out of bed won't get out of bed
won't   get   out   of   bed   don't   get   out   of bed
I'm like my sister   my brother   not a child waking before the dog
before the morning coffee had gone lukewarm

but that morning   mom's voice   *Get up. Go to your sister's room.*

a right turn   the long hallway   of the New Jersey-suburb-ranch-house
our Labrador yelling caution   I step across   red blue red blue   police lights breaking
through the kitchen   where we'd make cookies and bread and teriyaki chicken
bare feet   red then blue then red   the same spot
I broke my brother's nose
red then purple then yellow

perched on the edge of my sister's bed
      the place I read my first chapter book   I
learned
the number of words it takes to destabilize foundations

we lost the house.
the number of hours it takes to dismantle a household
six.

plasticky-adhesive-cardboard--whoosh-thwack-screech-slash
how to pack my boxes   how to understand
the last time   I'd count the stairs to the basement

steps I stumbled up 8 years old   shin running red
the gash the sand-art-glass bottle
broken under the table fort   mom's head whipping
help your sister!
mom can't stop the bleeding   her stomach churning

dad's delivery truck crammed to the tailgate   we say
goodbye to the blue pine
we planted after a Christmas   I was too young to
remember
the tire swing clings to the sycamore tree   mom's
daffodil bulbs remain buried

leaving the neighborhood   I didn't know   I'd lost the
first poem
I was proud of   or that the only snippet I remember
the line is number nine

will haunt me   like white aluminum siding   scared
oak floors   and faux-stone-linoleum

a motel parking lot   the family in one room
my fitful sleep saturated
the musk of maturing sweat   layered over   tacky-
flowered-synthetic-bedspread

mouth-open-breath-in-out-eyes-shut-ignore-blue-red-
blue-red-blue-red-inside-my-eyelids
go   to   sleep   go-to-sleep-go-to-sleep-go-to-sleep-
gotosleepgotosleepgotosleep

but when the house is gone   what's the home you
keep?

The Caretaker
by
Orla Fay

So easy to give into,
a usual pattern of thought,
actions repeated, signal sent,

a train in a long tunnel,
a blinkered horse,
a child punished,

continually belittled,
a tendency to anger quickly,
to feel trapped, petrified,

to shy away from approaching light,
to bolt at widening vision,
to shrivel against a gentle touch,

to come alive to salves and bandages,
to be beyond the point of repair,
the idea of ever blooming again

almost miraculous, suspicion present
in renewed watering, reluctance
in daily tending,

stopping and starting certain,
but hankering for better days,
and putting one foot in front of the other.

Leaving Connolly Station - *Dublin, July 2018*
by
Orla Fay

They call him Despair and inject
or commit – but he has many other names
and many reasons for existence
which the law cannot locate.
I've seen him held in a chokehold
against a McDonald's wall by society,
then pleaded for by a loyal lover, or brother.
I've seen his kind before, in paintings,
in Bacon's scream, most recently in print,
when teenager kills teenager.
But even winter could be beautiful,
another season, seed deep underground,
The Phoenix Park violet by lamplight,
bright eyes of a stag shining out from trees as snow fell.
And we might not have been in Dublin at all.
We could have been in Narnia or some other fairy-tale.

Hunger
by
Orla Fay

The aroma of frying food fosters appetite
and curiosity of origin, some primeval response coded –
the raising of a spear, the scattering of birds
on a wide sun-scorched plain, a tree, silhouette acacia
and a setting Serengeti sun, the going in for the kill
and later roasting wildebeest above a crackling fire,
dinner wafting all through the valley
beneath blackberry and pin-pricked pocketed sky,
ever changing and ever moving earth.

And here, now, in the bustling daylit city
a homeless man is cooking chicken nuggets
on a small propane stove by a wall
at the back of a row of houses.
Carefully he works, going from plastic bag
to plastic bag, baby wipes at the ready,
a paper plate and some sturdy cutlery
as a dishevelled crow, drunk in the heatwave
looks for a morsel.

His Jeans - (Villanelle)
by
Eimear Grace

In Dublin city amid a mild, gentle breeze
It's hard to imagine the things you might see
A man turned around and I noticed his jeans

Surely to God they were once bright blue denim
But for his jeans, I wouldn't remember him
In Dublin city amid a mild, gentle breeze

He was fumbling for nothing deep in his pockets
Almost blending with the rest of the homeless
A man turned around and I noticed his jeans

I wish that the image didn't follow me home
I did nothing about it, except write this poem
In Dublin city amid a mild, gentle breeze

He was mid to late fifties, unwashed and unkempt
His demeanour conveyed he'd rather be dead
A man turned around and I noticed his jeans

He stood out from the crowd, no regular fellow
His jeans were so soiled, they were actually yellow
In Dublin city amid a mild, gentle breeze
A man turned around and I noticed his jeans

A Priest, a prayer and a mutt named Jimmy
by
Helen Sullivan

One night as the clock struck 8:30 in the Brazen head pub. Patricia Donnelly and her faithful dog walked through its doors. Having never been in a public house before, Patricia stood for a moment to get her bearings. While she studied the pubs old and classic décor, she in turn was being studied by Mick the barman. Not because of her dog, who was allowed, providing he remained sitting on the floor and didn't bother anyone. But because Patricia neither looked like one of the many tourists that teemed daily through its doors or fitted the image of a local that was happy to visit a boozer.

When Patricia walked up to his bar and quietly ordered a pint of Guinness, Mick was stunned. Twenty-five years of working behind a bar had told him that Patricia was a glass of orange person, and not the kind that would readily engage in friendly chat. Which she confirmed by not uttering a word in response when Mick tried to strike up a conversation.

He also assumed that she would sit at one of the two tables not yet occupied and was surprised, when she chose to go instead and sit opposite the local priest, Father Daly. Now this puzzled Mick, as did her lifting her dog and putting him sitting on the seat next to her. Especially since, there was a big notice above her head, stating, no dogs allowed on the seats. She also then removed a ceramic bowel from her bag and placed it in front of her dog.

Under normal circumstances, Mick would not have hesitated to inform her of such rules. However, given that a weeklong festival of music and street entertainers were keeping the tourists away. Instead of enforcing the rules, on this occasion Mick let them slide. But fearing he may be wrong in his prejudgement of her not being a troublemaker. Mick decided that it was probably a good idea to keep an eye on Patricia.

With still a minute to go before Patricia's Guinness was ready to be served. Mick noticed that her fingers did an agitated drum upon the bowl. Naturally, Mick had thought her impatience was directed at him, and the two minutes wait, it took to execute a perfect pint. But when night after night Patricia visited the bar and continued to sit opposite the parish priest. Mick noticed that an angry glare accompanied the drilling of her fingers, and that both were aimed at Father Daly. Mick also observed, that though the tapping ceased on the delivery of the pint. The death stare remained.

Where other barmen were blind to subtle interchange and exchange between customers, Mick was not. After serval weeks of watching this odd behaviour and never seeing a word pass between Patricia or Father Daly. Confused and curious by the interplay of no dialog and puckering scowls from Patricia, as well as a continuous low growl from her dog.

One evening, no longer able to contain his curiosity, before Patricia left the bar and sat opposite Father Daly. Mick pulled her to one side and asked.

'Would you be so good as to tell me why for the love of God, do you come here night after night and stare at that poor priest?' To which, though hesitatingly at first, Patricia told him a tale that was both tragic and unbelievable. When she was done, in all of Mick's long years as a barman, and the many tales he had listened to, and of those he had eavesdropped on. Mick had never heard one quite like this.

For you see. Patricia's woes had begun when her husband Jimmy had got a bad doze of the runs. Though he had taken, over-the-counter remedies, nothing had work. As the days went by and her husband's condition had worsened, in the hopes that he would be able to clear her husband's gippy stomach. Patricia had called the doctor.

Unfortunately, the medication the doctor had prescribed only served to intensify the looseness of his bowels. At her wits end and with her husband Jimmy's condition growing worse by the day. Patricia, despite neither she nor her husband were church goers, and as unfavourable as the idea was to her at having a priest in her home. Patricia had reached out to Father Daly, who had not hesitated to pay them a visit.

That one visit became a nightly occurrence, whereupon his arrival, Patricia would offer Father Daly a cup of tea (which at that time had been his preferred beverage. Once his cup had been drained of every drop and his hands washed to lay them on Jimmy. Father Daly would then say aloud prayers for the sick.

Patricia and her husband Jimmy had thought that the prayers were healing him. For Jimmy had told Patricia when Father Daly had left after his first visit. That he felt as if something was beginning to change inside him. Needless to say. Patricia had been delighted and had been willing to accept that maybe there had been some truth to the power of prayers.

With renewed faith Patricia and her husband had thrown themselves wholeheartedly into the recited petitions and blessings from Father Daly. And it was on the evening of the tenth day that for the first time in three weeks. Patricia and her husband Jimmy had slept soundly.

After a night of unbroken sleep, early the next morning Patricia had been woken by what she described, as a rather hairy chin nuzzling the back of her neck.

Believing it was her Jimmy feeling fully rested and had got his zing back. Patricia had turned towards her frisky husband. Only to discover that it had not been Jimmy doing the nuzzling but a strange dog lying next to her. Not only that, but the dog had been dressed in her husband's blue stripe pyjamas.

With no sign of her husband and convinced it was some sort of trick, as Jimmy had been known to be a practical joker. Patricia had waited for him to return. After twenty minutes of there still being no sign of him and every room in her house had been searched. Patricia found to her horror that her husband had vanished. At that point, frantic with worry Patricia had rung friends and family but none had seen or heard from her Jimmy. And with a mysterious stray dog to contend with, once again, Patricia had turned to Father Daly.

Now Patricia was particularly adept at sussing out when something was wrong or not as it should be. So, when Father Daly had arrived with new reading glasses in his hand (glasses that had only been delivered that morning) Patricia had felt it in her bones that something was not quite right. For, not once during the ten days he had visited them had Father Daly worn glasses.

Trusting her gut feeling. Patricia had watched Father Daly open his prayer book and remove his bookmark from a page. A page that Patricia had recognized as the final blessing administered to her husband. She had also noticed that Father Daly had done so only after he had thrown her a sidelong glance out of the corner of his eye. All of which, had only pressed upon Patricia that she had been right in her assumption that something was amiss.

When perspiration had begun to ooze from every pore of Father Daly's body. Patricia had decided it was time to confront Father Daly. Following which, Father Daly had then confessed to Patricia that he had struggled to see the text. And that with his new bifocals resting snuggly upon his nose, had realised that not only had he misread the passage but also its title. In short, he had not blessed her husband with prayers for the sick, but with prayers for ailing animals. Which according to Father Daly had resulted in his prayers going seriously awry.

Now Patricia had had no idea how incorrect prayers could have brought about her husband's disappearance. She had said as much to Father Daly, who then had told Patricia that in addition to his mistake, a new moon phrase had begun on the first night he had visited her. And that in turn had caused Father Daly to be responsible for Patricia's husband, no longer being around.

There was seldom a time when Patricia could recall being left speechless, but at that moment she had been. She did not believe in astrology any more than she did, in the man in the moon. And even though she had thought she was about to be fed a cock-and-bull story. Patricia had remained silent and paid attention to Father Daly's explanation.

What Patricia had learnt that day, was that during a lunar cycle the universe invites those that are seeking a change to ask for a recourse or reset of their life. And that due to the combination of Father Daly's bad eyesight, the arrival of a new moon, a wrong prayer and Father Daly's good intentions while praying. An unwanted seed had been sowed on that very first night.

To summarize. Father Daly had blessed Jimmy with prayers for sick animals and that somehow amid it all, a request had been sent for a change, to which the universe had answered. A change that came to fruition ten days later at the end of the phrase and the rise of a full moon. And had resulted in the outer form of Jimmy's physical existence being completely transformed into that of a dog. Father Daly had then proclaimed that the mutt was to all intent and purposes Patricia's husband Jimmy.

Needless to say. Patricia had laughed it off as being a preposterous idea that the strength of a few prayers and a full moon could turn a human into a dog. But over the course of the following week. Patricia had come to realized, that the mutt she had woken to nuzzling her neck was indeed her husband.

Patricia's story was so incredulous and far-fetched that when she was finished telling it. Mick was sure it must have come straight from the pages of a paranormal mystery. When he said as much to her, to lend proof to her story Patricia produced a photograph where she pointed out a scar in the shape of a heart on Jimmy's left arm. To which she then lifted her little mutt, who Mick only noticed had a name plate inscribed with the name Jimmy as well as a scar in the shape of a heart on the side of his left leg.

Not only that, but in the photograph, it was plain to see that Jimmy had one blue eye and one brown eye, just like Patricia's little mutt. However, as Mick studied the photograph, he recognized Jimmy and recalled that every two weeks he used to come in for a pint of Guinness. And only now realized he had not seen him in a while. At first Mick dismissed it as just a coincidence that Patricia's husband and her mutt shared the same scar. To prove he had been told a tall tale. Mick took to his phone and googled dogs' eye colouring and discovered it could be a rare eye condition in her dog.

Before Patricia went and sat opposite Father Daly. Mick told her in a few well-chosen words that she was nothing more than a bully and a louse. To which she replied. 'Is that so, well, you tell me then why I waste my time coming here night after night?' He could not. Patricia was a complete mystery to him. Plus, that was the most words Patricia had spoken to Mick outside of her story.

With no reason to believe that what she had told him was not the truth, other than it being utterly impossible. Mick continued to study Patricia and her mutt over the coming weeks. It became apparent to him, that the dog had as much a dislike for Father Daly as Patricia had. He also discovered that Patricia's dog drank most of the Guinness and even wiped his upper lip with his paw, when he had finished supping from his bowl. Something he had observed Patricia's husband doing after each sip that he took.

Furthermore, when Mick asked people at Sunday service if they knew Patricia and Jimmy. Those that did, confirmed that the day Jimmy went missing, Patricia had found herself a dog. Which just so happened to be the very same day that Father Daly had taken to the booze and walked through the doors of the Brazen Head pub.

The Mighty Camac
by
Helen Sullivan

From the Dublin mountains to Heuston Station you wind
your way through
And though over the years parts of you have become
hidden.
It's in Corkagh Park where I take delight,
as each season your beauty changes.
Springtime brings green shoots along your banks.
And April showers fall with a soft tinkle upon your head.
The Summer's Sun, shimmering upon your cool waters
leaves me speechless.
For on a warm hazy day, there are no words to describe
your beauty.
And then comes Autumn and toppling leaves, tumbling
gracefully upon your surface.
Colours of green, orange and gold, gently being swept
along.
Then last, but not least, Winters fair snow.
Your waters dusted with tiny white flakes that say a
quick hello.
You are all this and so much more, your splendour far
beyond what I can express.
Throughout the years, although the land has changed,
you continue your wandering quest.
And on days that I am quite and still, I allow my mind to
wander.
I ask myself, if only you could speak,
What memories would you be willing to share?
Would you first tell with honour and pride?

How you helped build industries alongside your side.

Or perhaps you might prefer to speak,

of the shimmering fish that pass beneath.

Or would it be of the dragonfly's,

that flitter from reed to reed.

But then again, perhaps I am wrong, and it is the common frogs,

That hide in the lush grass of the ponds you have borne along the way.

Maybe its them, that gives you the most joy.

Perhaps, I am being stupid and foolhardy in my thinking,

that you would only speak of the joyous occasions.

If I do so, I apologize, for I like you are old now,

With each passing year I have found myself become sombre

I do not understand this world that has turned on its axle,

Where people dump their filth to pollute your depths and blight your beauty.

It makes me hang my head in shame.

But I have heard a plan is afoot to rid you of such poisonous waste.

Good news, I imagine you would say.

Alas though, I fear the world would have to turn another axle,

Before you, the time-honoured Camac and I, will ever see that day.

Not One Of Those Favoured
by
Helen Sullivan

When I was young, there would always be a Bing Crosby record playing on my granddad's PS record player, whenever I went to visit him. His favourite tune was 'When Irish Eyes Are Smiling' and not a word would he, nor I, be allowed to utter until the last note finished. By the time I was six years old I knew that damn song inside out. Now, I can barely remember a line or two.

The reason my granddad loved Bing was because his family had come from Ireland and according to my granddad, that song and the other Irish songs he recorded was a tribute to the Emerald Isle. Now, as a young kid this was a big mystery to me. I couldn't get my head around why a yank that had not been born in Ireland wanted to sing Irish songs, particularly since I wasn't much keen on them myself. My granddad said it was because his family had never forgotten their roots, even so, I went to Disneyland when I was five, which was the best ever, but I knew I wouldn't be singing songs about America when I grew up, and when I had pointed this out to my granddad his reply to me had been, 'Why would ya, there's nothing memorable about those yanks, not like us Irish who are known to be a friendly and helpful bunch.' My granddad filled my head with tales of what life was like when he was growing up, of how people helped each other. He was immensely proud of being Irish and he genuinely believed we were a nation that would never turn away a stranger in their time of trouble.

To that I now say, 'what a load of horseshit', an expression that my granddad favoured just as much as he did ole Bing, especially when someone's opinion differed to his, which was almost as frequent as the utterance. And maybe in the time my granddad spoke about, we were a nation more tolerant and possibly even helpful, towards the displaced with no fixed abode. But not in this century. I now realize that my granddad like most old people romanticize about the past, they prefer to hold onto only their good memories of Dublin City and leave out the bad. My granddad was my hero, and I believed his tales of what Dublin was like in the 'rare auld times', as he used to say, and for a long time because of his teachings, I too wore those same rose-tinted glasses.

My blinkers are gone, and I am no longer economical with the truth regarding those very same streets my granddad fondly spoke about. For I have encountered little, or no kindness towards the homeless in our not so fair isle, except maybe from the charitable organisations that have sprung up all over the place. No, the only smiling eyes I've ever seen, are for the yanks who spend their tightly held dollars in the overpriced cafes of Temple Bar, because they certainly do not smile on the down-and-outs dossing in the many doorways of our two-faced city.

On the streets, greetings are for friends meeting up on a night out, they're not for the destitute sleeping rough. Yet the homeless are all tarnished with the same brush, regardless of there being many different reasons why the friendless are without a place to call their own. If I were to tell you, that no one ever makes a conscious decision to be homeless, but that sometimes one's own decisions can have an impact that one could never have imagined happening to them. And that this especially applies to the young who thankfully, many are fortunate to come through unscathed from their mistakes, while others are not so lucky, and end up on a path where a future took for granted is lost to them. Would you believe me. If you don't, you're a fool, because I am proof that if you turn left, when you should have turned right, that there is no going back

You see, I was not one of those favoured youths who came through their mistakes intact, and six years ago at the age of eighteen, what was supposed to be a night of fun ended up being one that would very quickly rob me of my life. That was in the year 2014 and I was out celebrating my leaving cert results, a whopping 595 points. I was wild with excitement; it had been more than enough to get me into Trinity. I was on my way to doing a single honours degree in Law and Political science, and if my life had gone as planned, I would have been the first person in my family's history to go on to third level education. Which had been a big deal, because not only had it been my dream but also my mother's and father's.

Like all other teenagers I believed I was invincible, all my hard work had earned me the right to party, but I had not counted on crack cocaine being my downfall. Shit, my friends had been snorting it for the past year and a half while I had spent the time studying, and they could take or leave it. I had partying to catch up on and within five minutes of entering Copper Face Jacks, a club on Harcourt St, I was having my very first taste of crack cocaine. I was alive and buzzing and I was indestructible, and the world was there for me to take.

Now, I won't bore you with the details of how it went from being only a weekend high, to it very quickly becoming a daily need. Instead, I will jump forward to four years later and 2018 or to be more accurate, Wednesday the 28th of February. In case you have forgotten, that was the year the 'Beast from the East' paid Ireland a visit. It was also to become one of the worst and one of the best years for me living on the streets.

In a life before crack, my friends who were no longer my friends used to call me 'Bull' on account of my stocky build. But by then my body no longer resembled what my nickname implied. The cocaine had robbed me of my want and ability to eat, because that is what it does, and beneath the padding of my clothes I was nothing more than skin and bone. The only thing I craved was the short release the drug gave me. It had rotted and decayed my teeth and had placed deep crevice's in my face that truly should only belong to a man in his forties and not, in a face that was barely twenty-three-years-old. Shit, my own mother if she had ever passed me by on the street would have continued on walking and not only because she would have failed to recognize me, but also, because I had caused her and the rest of my family considerable pain.

The day before the 'Beast' arrived I had muscle spasms ripping into my stomach, it felt as if something was trying to pull my insides apart, and as it had been a few hours since my last hit, I had spent the best part of the day visiting all my old haunts trying to score. But the streets had been empty. Emergency bedding had been issued by the Minister for housing, for the forthcoming storm, and the do-gooders were out herding us into shelter before it hit. My take on that had been, the additional shelter was a means for the government to ease their conscience, big bloody deal, seeing that every year 40 to 50 of us die out on the streets, and because the country was in storm crisis, it had taken the bleeding 'beast' to put the skids under them.

Now I know, without the government and the best part of the population coming out and saying it to my face. Those of us that live rough are deemed to be little better than the vermin that blight their precious city. You can disagree all you want, but we have shitheads every week romping around the city spitting and urinating on us while we sleep, that tell us so. And yes, maybe some of us warrant the peoples need to rid us of the streets and looking back, if a better version of me had existed, he would have dumped my sorry ass over the Liffey wall. Because I'm ashamed to say, I had become the worst sort of human being there was, the sort, that would have done anything to feed his habit.

I can't deny and nor will I deny that I have in the past, inflicted pain and violence upon the unsuspecting public to get what I needed. I had even on one or two occasions sliced through flesh when cutting through the strap of a handbag. And if it had ever come to it, I know I would not have hesitated to murder for it. This, I do not confess easily.

But here is a newsflash, not everyone on the streets is like me. Many are there because they have no other option open to them. If you care to look close enough, you will come across runaway kids as young as twelve trying to fend for themselves on the streets, for one reason only, and that is that life is preferable here than to the one at home. There are also old age pensioners that you believe to be tramps, who have lost love ones and are there counting down their days in alleyways on account that their grief would not allow them to remain in a place that reminded them of what was gone. Then there are those who have lost jobs and are no longer able to keep up the payments of a home, and feel that they have no option but to see the streets as the only dwelling available to them. So make no mistake, we are all out there, and the next time you pass someone like me on the street with your nose in the air, remember, there is nothing written anywhere that says it can't happen to anyone at any given time. So, take a moment to ponder on that.

Well, that took an unexpected turn and now with my speech over, it's time to get back to my story. For various reasons, there were a few like me unable to settle behind four walls that refused the beds being offered. We used the cloak of darkness to disappear like ghosts into the underbelly of the streets that had become deserted by the threat of the beast. Even the rodents had taken cover. However, there had still been a few Garda patrols rounding up those they had missed earlier, and a bunch of us who usually crashed down by the fish market cleared our stuff out before we got nabbed. Some headed towards Smithfield hoping to score there, but I had decided to try my luck on Georges street.

With the full extent of my worldly possessions on my back, a sleeping bag given to me by an inner-city organization and a backpack that contained two needles, a spoon, a bottle of water, a lighter, an old brillo pad and pipe. Now you may be scratching your head as to why I would have a brillo pad and pipe, well let me explain. I used cocaine in every form possible. I snorted, I smoked, I ingested, and I used them to smoke the crack before I got into injecting it. And I held onto them because I never knew when they might come in handy. I also had a squashed Mars bar, for when I felt hungry.

I stayed clear of the main streets and darted through the back lanes and alleyways until I came to Capel Street, where I ended up meeting a Moroccan guy dealing on the corner. Now Tony and Rory Fletcher were my normal dealers, and Capel Street was their patch, and I knew, buying off the newcomer saw little chance of neither him nor myself living past Friday. I said as much to the big Moroccan who told me that the Fletchers and his associates had been grassed up and busted the night before. I may be no better than the maggots under the earth but believe me when I tell you, that those two brothers were real scumbags and they deserved everything they got. The big Moroccan also told me Capel street was now his territory and that the Fletchers would be bothering no one anytime soon.

I hadn't been too sure about that, but at that moment in time I didn't give a flying fuck. Because, by then I was tense and edgy, my whole insides felt as if a rat had burrowed beneath my skin and was slowly eating me alive. Anyway, it must have been about three in the morning when I crossed over the bridge with my head bowed low against the freezing winds that had blowed crossways over the water. By now the weather was Baltic and I remember that there had been a real bite to it, it had nipped and snapped at the exposed flesh of my face and hands like some deranged and rabid dog. That and the fact that my need for the bag of coke stuffed into my jean pocket was fierce, made me decide to bed down on Dame street, except, I hadn't counted on the few doorways that were suitable, being taken.

Having said that, one of the doorways had been big enough for me to squeeze in, despite there being two lads already in it. What had stopped me from doing so was that I knew the two of them and they were right fuckers. They'd kicked the shit out of me a number of times and had robbed me of my geer, and even though the two of them were totally wasted, I decided not to risk it.

So, I continued walking towards Georges street where I had in the past laid my head a few times. To be honest, my plan was to crash in one of the alleyways, but I did what I always did whenever I passed by a gated entrance to a shop. I rattled the iron gates pulled across it on the off chance that one had been left unlocked, of course there never had been. Imagine my surprise when the gate on one swung open, not only that, but resting up against its door was a bunch of dry cardboard boxes flattened and tied together with string. After I had covered the tiled entrance with the cardboard and emptied the contents of my bag on top. I injected my blow and wrapped myself in the sleeping bag where, for a short while, everything had been right with the world. At that point, I had everything that I needed. But I hadn't banked on the snow that came soon after.

Snow, that when it came, came with no mercy. It covered every space available and begrudged anyone trying to claim some for their own. And when I awoke, I woke to a world even more hostile than before. The city was like a ghost town, not a sinner walked the streets that were iced and snowed over. I was lucky that that night the heavens had favoured me, I barely survived. Some of the others that had also chosen to remain outside had not been so charmed. They had their life stolen from them while they slept, smothered by the she devils white blanket that had frozen them to their marrow.

I dug out the two I had passed the night before in the doorway on Dame Street, the one I had nearly considered bunking down in. It was not to revive them, but to strip them of their belongings. I walked away with a jacket, a hat, and a pair of leather gloves barely held together by its stitching. Let me remind you before you pass judgement, humanity does not pound the pavements, the lost, the broken and the cursed do. I had known that the wheel of fortune would not spin twice, luck would not come my way for a second time and the way I saw it, the owners of the items I removed were gone, they no longer had a use for them whereas I did.

That day the streets remained deserted. Most of the shops did not open and the absence of people lent an eerie silence to the air. It was as if the city were expecting an apocalypse of pale horsemen to come and dole out the Lords punishment to any that dared to walk upon his white land. And it certainly felt as if Gods right hand had fallen, as the winds and snow continued. I took my chances in the Phoenix Park. I thought there would have been more cover with the trees and what not, but I had been wrong, snow drifts made it near impossible to walk or find a sheltered spot. But eventually I came across an area of trees and hedgerows, and I used my gloved hands to tear away at the inside of one of the hedges.

All the while I had been attacking the hedge, I had ignored a soft whine that had carried in the wind. It was obviously some wounded creature, but the only thing that had been on my mind was getting myself out of the wind and snow that had been using me as its whipping boy and into my thorny hideaway. When I had an opening big enough for me to fit and curl into, I arranged my backpack and sleeping bag in the hopes that they would protect me against its thorny branches.

But once inside, though the howl of the wind had been softened, the cry had not. A cry that continued until I could no longer brush aside the infernal sound that had waged war upon my ears and brain. I went in search of what I had imagined to be a hedgehog or some other odious critter that lived in the undergrowth, and had not been prepared for the piteous soul that I found tied to a bush. A little three-legged-dog with the largest ears I had ever seen.

I assure you that the streets are cruel, cruel beyond imagination, this I know. And I am not saying that my addiction was an excuse for my behaviour. Yes, I have sinned, and my transgressions will not go unpunished, but I cannot help questioning how someone without reason could have abandoned a dumb animal to die a slow and agonising death. Is that not just as despicable as the way in which I have lived. I believe it is. I did not have it in me to end that little dog's life, which had been my intention on finding the injured creature. Instead, I untied him and brought him with me into my thorny bunker, where I held him tight beneath my jacket, and he in turn, licked my face with gratitude. It had been the first bit of physical contact I had had with another living soul in an awfully long time, and it had felt good.

Though time was short for my friend and I, we did not cry in the dead of night when death came to slay us with his icy hand. For he did us a favour. He freed us from this heartless land.

Now you may recall that I said 2018 was both the worst and the best year of my life living on the streets. I feel I should explain. The best, because I found the only friend during my time there and despite the coldness of the day, I had been filled with love and warmth. Together, that dog and I were cocooned in snow until someone came and found us, which was three days later. And the worst, which you may say is death, but for me it was not. It was the worst because, after we had both found one another our friendship only lasted for one more day.

According to Focus Ireland in the week 21st to 27th September 2020 there were 8,656 homeless people across Ireland.

The Hand Shake
by
Patricia Kane

The whispers of the grieving congregation were not all about the dear departed. For those who lived and shared the past with the deceased, their whispers were of whether or not he, the ex-husband would show his face?

Their curiosity was satisfied when, as the priest came onto the altar to begin the ceremony, the double doors at the back of the church opened. Every head turned.

Chris couldn't help enjoying his grand entrance. It would give the town's busy bodies fodder for a long time to come. His show of bravado weakened when his eyes locked on the lone coffin in front of the altar. If somebody had tried to convince him that a lifetime of memories could flood a mind in a brief moment, he would have dismissed them as spoofers or drunken idiots or both.

She had been the biggest prize in the town in those days. Her pick of any fella who tipped his hat her way. He remembered the power of his want for her. He also remembered that his want was simply because every man wanted her and none had managed to snare her.

He remembered the feel of her small soft hand in his when he was introduced to her and his matter a fact attitude about the introduction. He knew that given the amount of attention she received from other men, his off handedness would catch her interest.

The sweetness of making her his own lasted until the end of their first year of marriage.

He should never have done that to her, made her a challenge, but as someone had recently pointed out to him that he had eventually set her free. Free to find a love she deserved.

He let the double doors close softly and walked quietly towards the man who had made her happy. He knew that every eye in the church was on him as he walked towards the front pew. He placed his hand on her coffin then turned and offered his right hand to her grieving husband.

His hand hung in the air. Chris could feel the intense silence of the packed church.

Unbeknown to those present, he had made a point of seeking out her grieving husband the night before in private. And after a surprisingly comfortable meeting they both agreed that the woman they'd both married would love an unforgettable funeral.

So, they'd come up with the grand entrance and the pausing of the shaking of each other' hand.

Chris waited.

Loving Dublin
by
Natasha Helen Crudden

From the wind-torn hilltop
I survey the south valley
All the way to the mountains

Salt air, whole and uncut
By the screech of sirens and the wail of car alarms

This is where you'll find me
When the trees blaze a fire glow upon the sky
Or down among the rivers and roses
Or sprinting over grassbanks and woodland paths

Perchance you'll find me
Lingering at Islandbridge
Idling upon the Liffey
Or on the trail of stags at Phoenix Park
Antlers bowed
I revere this majesty and walk on, humbled
By how insignificant I am in it all

This is truly loving Dublin
Not the weekly pilgrimage
To the latest
hipster – vegan – gluten-free – Prosecco – flavour of the
month
This is real Dublin, pure Dublin
The Dublin that keeps on giving
It isn't brunch with the girlos or cans with the lads
South-east of Dame Street

Where everyone knows
Droppin' the G
Denotes hipness

Jets firing skyward
From stone-carved fountains
The scurry of squirrels
Up branches of chestnut trees
That huddle close
Shudder in the wind
and drop their conkers
Sleek mahogany born of hedgehog shells

The mirror calm of the canal
Before it sweeps into the lock,
Cascades into a *meerschaum*
Then slows, shimmers and emerges as a stillframe
Further downstream

You'll find me there
Where the rush of the breeze
And patter of raindrops on tangerine leaves
Drown out the city din
Where the sky and the mountains
Unfurl to conceal
Neon signs that testify
To craft beer and doughnuts, burritos and haircuts
And frappe – lattu – cinnos
Just the way you like 'em

This is where you'll find me
This is where I'll be

A Lost Curlew
For Dianna Bartone
by
Alan O'Brien

A weather-slab of ice-cold atmosphere descended on Dublin town. Bringing with it a sporadic fog, so deep in parts it plumed visibly and voluptuously in the air. It was very early in the morning. The traffic had dwindled to un-noticable. Freddie *Readybrek* Carpenter trod down the boardwalk along Ormond Quay with a rolled-up-sleeping-bag-bag swinging merrily in one hand and a plastic bag with cans and bread in the other.

He concentrated momentarily on a strange sound. A repetitive piping-wailing sound. A haunting sound it was. Freddie thought 'banshee', noncommittally, then decided it was an animal of some sort, a bird perhaps. Looked into the plumes of fog, a whistle, his own version of the sound, piped from his lips. It fell dead. It sounded wrong to him. Down to Four Courts he headed. Nice & private it was these days, he thought, and a brave view of the river too.

Freddie followed the granite wall that snakes the banks through the city, and passed the emptied Ormond Hotel. He yearned ever slightly at the deserted silence it exudes. Just like the silence of his cabin at night. Down behind Sherriff Street. A watchman's cabin for an old live cattle-stores. With little stove. Dry. Nice & private too.

When Freddie got away from the home nowhere was home. But that cabin, that nearly was. Took a little while at first. Children threw stones, called him names. Told them his name is Freddie. Called him Benny. Didn't like that, those sky pilots were bennies, not him! (No no, no not to be thinked about no more no) Didn't react against the kids' taunts though. Just kept himself to himself. After a while, a year or so, kids' Ma's were sending over small pots of coddle in the winter.

-Ma's afraid you'll freeze to death, they'd sometimes say.

Freddie told them about *Readybrek*, how it made him glow. And, inadvertently re-baptised himself. Freddie *Readybrek*. That was the 1980s. Then the drugs were got. Freddie watched kids grow up to kill themselves. And turn against their very own worlds. They invaded his cabin. Took it over to go about the killing themselves. But, local men came and got it back for him. Told them 'definitely not there, that's Freddie *Readybrek*'s cabin!' Sacred place...to some, seemed. Then...the developers. And they just win. Wrecked the cabin! It was *their* nice & private place now. People shouted up for him. Freddie *Readybrek?* He just moved on.

Freddie made his bed. Plastic spread down, then sleeping bag. Nestled into the portico pillars of Four Courts looking out on to the Liffey. His breath plumed like the fog. He ruffled himself deeper into the sleeping-bag while opening a can of beer, and supped. Icicles, pointed accusingly down upon him from above.

A curlew, lost, calls out. It fearfully marvels at the strange hard-bright-dark jungle it has found. Sensing the sea close, it calls out louder. The curlew, hovers, then glides along, undulating; the Liffey as guide, seabound.

A Dog's Life
by
Paul Lee

Dermo got up from his patch outside the bank and went down a few doors to peer in the window of a shop that had a clock. Only 10 minutes left before the off licence closed. He cursed Boyle and counted his change for the umpteenth time. He had only made €3.60 in two hours. Enough for three cans of cider. This covid was hurting. Very few people around to tap and those that were around tended to steer clear of him. "Sorry, no change bud" was all he heard these days. No one seemed to have cash anymore. He found that he did slightly better if he wore a mask. He found one on the street earlier and once he had it on he started to get a few bob. But it was getting late. Boyle promised he would meet him before 10pm and they would share their spoils. But it was always the same these days. Boyle would bum enough to get drunk, forget about Dermo and fall asleep someplace.

He could not risk waiting any longer so he bought his cans and went in search of Boyle. Hopefully he would have had a bit more luck. He wandered down Camden Street towards Temple Bar checking doorways and lanes along the way. He checked around the Central Bank but no sign there. He spotted Mary but avoided her because she would want one of his precious cans. She would give him a wank for a can but he could not afford it with only three to see him through the night. He would keep them until he found somewhere to bed down for the night. It was October and it was cold but at least it was dry. They used to spend a lot of time around the Central Bank. That's where Boyle taught him the tricks you needed if you were to survive. Like how you had to get your clothing sorted first of all. You had to wear lots of light layers rather than a heavy coat. A heavy coat that got wet meant you were in trouble. Different layers and you could discard one or two and dry them out. They would often sleep around the bank in full public view, which he hated. But Boyle told him it was safer to sleep in a public place than somewhere secluded because if you were attacked you could call out for help.

No sign of Boyle in Temple Bar either so he crossed the Ha'penny bridge and headed towards Smithfield. The wind up the Liffey made him shiver and he wished he was drunk. He was hungry, sober and angry. The whole world seemed dead. There was no one around and not a butt to be found. He was too late for a hostel now and he had missed the soup run on Grafton Street. Boyle stopped going to soup runs because he was so scared of covid. He used to love meeting up with everyone in the Capuchin Centre on Bow St. but since covid it was takeaway only.

Boyle's favourite place for crashing at the moment was a derelict cottage on Chicken lane in Stoneybatter so he headed up there. He despised Boyle sometimes but they depended on each other. He hoped he would find him because he hated being on his own at night. It was always a worry. When they first hooked up he was only 23 and new to street life. Boyle was an old hand at it and over twice his age. He learned quickly that you have to have someone with you at night that you can trust. You sleep better and safer. Without these tips he would not have survived those early years. But these days Boyle would get so out of it he would forget his own rules. Now it was Dermo who did the caring.

They first met in the Phoenix Park when Boyle approached him and asked if he had seen a black and white collie. He explained how his dog had gone missing two days before. He was desperate to find him. Sparkie had kept him warm at night and looked out for him for the last three years. If anyone came near him while he slept Sparkie would bark and wake him up.

Dermo felt sorry for him and offered to help in the search. They ended up traipsing around Dublin for weeks looking for him. Then they became inseparable. Dermo just kinda took over from Sparkie. He became Boyle's new dog and like a dog if he was bold he could get a kick in the hole or a box on the ear. He got many of them but he was young and stupid then and was just out of the nick. When he had finished school he felt free at last, but he could not figure out who he was free to be. He had stayed at home for a few years but went kinda crazy. Gambling, stealing, lying and cheating on friend and foe. Started smoking weed and hash but soon was snorting coke or speed or smack. Anything to get him to somewhere he had never been. Everything went downhill rapidly until he ended up in Mountjoy for two years. When he got out his Dad would not let him back in the house. He reckoned his Da was afraid of him because he knew he couldn't punch him around the place anymore. That's when he met Boyle.

They had been together now almost 5 years, apart for a few weeks when he had stayed in a flat with Mary Lynch. In the early days Boyle and himself had travelled the country, sleeping in barns, hotel car parks, hospital waiting rooms, bus stations, fast food restaurants, you name it. They got on well enough but sometimes had terrible fights. Boyle could always give him a hammering. But they stayed together. In recent times the tide had turned and Dermo would come out on top. Boyle was not so strong anymore. The years of living like an animal on the street were starting to tell. He had been an alcoholic most of his life. He was married once and worked as a bus driver, but lost his job after driving a bus drunk. His wife had kicked him out soon after that.

He found Boyle on the cold floor of the cottage in Chicken Lane. He was asleep and wearing a mask. Dermo kicked him awake and shouted, "You said you would meet me on Camden Street ye bollix." Boyle struggled to wake. "Sorry, I fell asleep" he mumbled.

"Yea, you got what you wanted and forgot about me. Have you anything to drink?"

"Here". Boyle handed him a whisky bottle with a few mouthfuls left. Dermo took the bottle, knocked it back and opened a can of cider. "Thanks for keeping me a drop. Have you tobacco?" Boyle handed him tobacco and skins. Dermo rolled a fag. Boyle sat up and rolled one for himself. "Have you any more cider?" asked Boyle.

"Fuck off, said Dermo. All I collected was enough for three cans. You've had a bottle of whiskey. I don't know why I stick with you. All you do is look after yourself."

"Oh fuck off will you. You can go anytime you want" said Boyle, "I can manage on my own."

"Ah yea, you were always better than me at being a bum" said Dermo. "I still dream that things can be better, but you just get so fucken out of it you can't even dream anymore."

"That's your problem" said Boyle. "You keep dreaming. Maybe I'm the clever one because I accept I'm a fucken looser and that's my lot. And it's your lot as well, so just get used it. You think you are better than me then fuck off home to mammy and daddy, if they'll have you. You were never fit for the road anyway."

Dermo jumped up in a rage and kicked him in the side but his foot hit something hard. He looked down and saw another bottle of whiskey sticking out of Boyle's pocket. He reached down and grabbed it. "You selfish bastard" he shouted. Boyle staggered to his feet. "That's mine, it's for tomorrow. Give it back to me". Dermo pushed him onto the floor and kicked him several times. Boyle curled up to shield the blows. That was all he did these days. Just curled up and took it. Dermo put the bottle to his mouth and gulped heartily. Boyle just lay there motionless.

After ten minutes of silence Dermo started to sob. "Now see what you've done. You always make me so mad. Why do you do it? Why do you have to say those horrible things to me"? Sure I dream. I dream of Mary Lynch. Remember her? After the accident she looked after me. She healed my cuts and bruises and calmed my crazy fucken head. And then I got the money. Five thousand euro. I could have stayed with her but I kept coming back to look after you. But all you wanted was for me to spend it on drink. If I didn't you screamed at me and screamed at everyone on the street. Standing in front of the traffic and screaming about how I'd robbed you. How I owed you cause you looked after me like a son. You kept screaming until I went and got drink or gave you more money. So we drank it all. Nothing to show for it after a few months but a pair of shoes. Five thousand fucken euro. And then Mary wouldn't even speak to me. Wouldn't let me back in the flat. Thrown out onto the street again. That was your fault. I could have had a life with Mary. A home with clean sheets and a warm bed. But you just wanted me to spend it all on drink. You were happy then, weren't you? Happy I was back being a bum just like you."

"She left because you got drunk and hit her, nothing to do with me" said Boyle.

"That's a lie you bastard" Dermo shouted as he stood up and kicked Boyle again several times. Boyle just stayed curled up in a ball, his hands covering his head.

Dermo moved away and sat down on a cement block. He drank in silence. He knew Boyle was right. He had got drunk and punched Mary when she complained about him wasting his money and coming back to the flat pissed. He knew he had blown his chance of a different life and it hurt him bad. He started sobbing like a child.

"Now you've made me feel guilty again. You always make me feel guilty. It's your fault I behave like this. You say horrible things and try to keep everything for yourself"

"God forgive you" mumbled Boyle.

"I'm afraid of God" Dermo sobbed. "What will he say to me? He will ask me why I kicked you. Why I hit people who tried to help me. And he won't let me in either. Why should he? I'm just like a dog on the street. Hell can't be this bad, can it?"

He took a can of cider from his pocket and went over to Boyle. "Here, have some cider". Boyle did not answer.

"Here for fucks sake, I'm sorry. I was fucken freezing and waiting for you for hours. I'm sorry".

He shook Boyle, "look, here's your whiskey, come on. Boyle, answer me".

Mad World
by
Anthony Carty

Clouds of destiny are so hard to find
Roaring blues seas are one of a kind
Mountains and fields spoiled by our vanity
But who is there to reclaim our sanity
The man above sits in his chair
Dictates the orders that so unfair
War rages on as the man insists
Cruelty and suffering lurks in the mist
Tormentual crisis forms anxiety plus uncertainty
Unchecked notes reflects swivelling captured calmity
Famine and disease is all around
Is there a solution that can be found
Extremity of people is forever dying
Does anyone listen to the children crying
Nature calls at the door to take away human existence
The way the world consumes itself nature attends to the difference
Fed up and bored of population games of domain
Listen, take a walk, consider, come back sometime with refrain
There is something else needed to, to make a new revelation
Time is up, must go, the conundrum values swing creation
Your chapter has expired - leave elongated pages on the table - chop chop, off you pop - and disappear

Homeless
by
Andrea Lovric

"Country road, take me home, to the placeeee I belooonnnggg…"
Looking down at her half melted, unfinished strawberry daiquiri, Jade didn't even realise the full blast speakers and all voices fused into a what she could only describe as an ear infection feeling that was specific to this very song in every country west of the Black sea. She was too busy looking at her sparkly silver wannabe Kim Kardashian dress, minus the butt. Short enough for Jade to be very careful how she would reach for her jacket, which of course, was too thin to keep anyone warm and was of course, only warn as and accessory, yet still long enough to be perfectly okay for her to go out in and also be pretty fashionable, cause #fashionista #bestnighever.

However, the only thing she actually was, was Kimmo de Grafton Street. When actually, she lived in James. Worst of all she wasn't even from James. Or Dublin. She was just living here.

OMG, this song again! She thought. *Take me home? What home? I don't even have a home. Sure, I have a place to stay. That I pay rent for. A huge amount also, but that's a completely different conversation. So, yes, I have an apartment. Don't forget my 3 housemates. And then there is my parents' house. But which one of those is home, huh? I guess I don't have one.*

Fekin' song. Fekin'?? When did I start saying fekin'? It's not just the lack of home, I don't even have my personality anymore. At least not here. There are 2 of me. Jade no1 and Jade no2. Multiple nationalities Jade. Multiple homenalities Jade.

Jade stood up, reaching for her jacket and purse. Very carefully, remember?

- Hey, where ye going?
- I'm gonna head home, guys.

There I said it – home. Let's laugh about it and go on with our lives. She thought.

- Ah, come on, don't be a party pooper, one more drink and we go to McDonalds! Gemma said, while reaching for her bazillioned drink.
- Wooooo, West Virgniaaaaaaa!!!!
- No, I'm just tired. She lied.
- Right, suit yourself! Talk tomorrow!

Walking down to take a taxi, Jade could not get rid of this song. Firstly, because it's annoyingly catchy and second, because she was thinking about this home thing a bit too much.

I don't understand. When I'm here, I miss my hometown. I miss the streets, the bars, the parks. I miss going out in jeans. Yeah, what happened to that? Going on a night out in jeans and a nice top? I miss my home. Whenever I book a flight, get so excited and then when I'm there-nothing. It doesn't feel like home anymore. The town is mine, but it's not. I know it, but I don't know it, you know? And then I miss Dublin and I want to go to this home. In both countries, I say I have a flight home, when referring to the other one. But which one really IS my home? I don't feel like I belong in neither of them.

When will I feel like a town is mine again? Will this feeling ever come back?

Jade could not decide if she was angry or sad at this point. She felt like crying, but also like going back in time and warn herself that this would happen. But then she thought that old Jade probably wouldn't have listened anyway. So she started laughing at herself. Thankfully the group of people on the street she was approaching were too far away to realise.

Ah, there, a taxi! Her train of thought got interrupted.

- Heya!
- Heya, missus! Where to?
- James, please.

The taxi driver turned on the car and the radio turned on automatically.

What was playing, you ask? "Country road, take me home…"

Oh, for fucks sake! She thought, when the driver was delighted and started humming to it.

Just, shut up, what home? I feel homeless.

Before
by
Nancy Matchton Owens

It could be me, sitting over there, like you,
crouched on the wet pavement.
I never meet your eyes and
I don't want to know.
My life is too important.
I cannot afford to acknowledge you.
You and your desperation
You and your vacant stare and matted hair
What I fail to see is your life was important too; before

Before you were forced to sleep rough
Before you were part of a family
A group that loved you
Before you washed yourself
And walked a dog.
Before you drove a lovely car
Before you were
left to unravel.
left to beg.
Something you stuck your nose up at a long time ago
and now are doing on a daily basis. It does not amount to
much, because nobody has change.
Hungry in a pandemic.
Hungry without one.

Before you were fit and strong and ran marathons
Before you were backed onto a corner

Before you had to do something that you knew was
beneath you
Before you couldn't live with the thoughts and could not
afford to tell anybody
You had lost your grip.
Before you were
Left to decay and wither.
Left to the elements like dead leaves.
One day you had shelter.
Next day you shivered on a box next to where you
relieved yourself.
Society peddling along and doesn't know the half of it,
eh?
We live beside each other like parallel lines.
One alive, one existing
We forget we are one step away from debt.
We forget we are at the hands of another to hire or fire
us.
Our lives are in society's hands as to whether we
Are looked after or let fall by the wayside, into oblivion.
We are a step away from the landmine erupting.

It could be me, sitting over there, like you
Before the world carried on and stopped caring.

It could be me, sitting over there,
Even if I tried my best.
What happened before is faraway now.
It could be me, sitting over there, like you,
Crouching on the wet pavement
Down and out

Sunny Glow
by
Faith Malone

I had to run to help her
We went for a fake tan but came back paler
I just wanted the night to be over
Cigarette air that's snowy silver
Happy to anxious
Then back again
Then home
To freshen up
to a sunny glow
A sunny glow called home.

For Anybody...
by
Robert Smyth

What have I done, what good?
I can't remember, I hope I do soon.
Yes, I see the homeless man's eyes..
I see through the many lies.
He looks at me, "Lucky and then some." He says.
With a collection of cider bottles and a meaningless grin.
Dark, sullen fluid runs through his groin,
He holds out an ice-blue hand in question,
His expression ignored and cleared with a coin.
For anybody to see, to understand, to give, to comprehend.

Consequences
by
Órla Gately

Months of worry in sections
slices compared.
It's easier to forget the forgotten
now we're hidden.
Numbers mean less when they have to travel
The cry rings out 'nowhere to go'
Empty path, time not walking past.
No change.
As we all wait for what we need.

Splitting seeds
by
Victoria Gilbert

Dedicated to nature and that
And human nature has a roof over its head and that
So dedicated to that
To create space between nature and this
The family tree is the root of nature it is
Friends can put your love for nature in it
Contributing to nature with it
When your splitting seeds.

There Is No Them And Us
by
Ann Herkes

There is No them and Us
it's a We
We are no different
Don't you see?
Each and every one of us
We need to
Pee
We need to
Shit
We need to eat
We need to breathe
We need Company
We need to be believed
To be safe and seen
To be cuddled
and
comforted
We all have
the same
Needs
It's not a them and Us
it's a We
We need to see
that when we hurt
that hurt
is the same
for each of us
Each and everyone one

of us cuts and bleeds
We need empathy
To connect
The Dots
To understand
It's not them and Us
Life is unpredictable
Not linear
Nor
Safe and Secure
It's not a Them and Us
Tomorrow could be
the day
Your little Empire
turns to dust
Then US
becomes a
THEM
Isolated,
Shamed
 Fallen from Grace
because
US made a status out of
BEING
HUMAN
It's not Them and Us
Labels are so limiting
So disconnecting
Know yourself
Know and relate to
Other
HUMAN

BEINGS
It's not a Them and Us
It's
A
WE.

The Three Latchicos
by
Liam Kennedy

It was on a dreary Saturday night
And a shower of rain came down
I was walking up Ballyfermot Road
After spending all me money in town
I was jumped on by three Latchicos
When I was nearly home
There was two of them came from Landen Road
And one from Garryowen

Well the first one kicked me in the back
The next one in the head
I fell down like an aul wet sack
Sure I thought that I was dead
Then the third one kicked me in the side
I said now that's a shame
If I had [*****] here   [Pick   a   name   from   present
company]
Yis wouldn't play that game

Well then I jumped up to me feet
I said you've gone too far
I threw yer man across the street
And he got hit by a stolen car
His mates ran out to help him
But they didn't know the score
They got knocked down by a Honda
That was robbed in Inchicore

So no more they'll jump on decent men
That's walkin home alone
For they spent three weeks in James' St
Before they were let go home
'cause when that terrible night was o'er
Three men had broken bones
There was two of them came from Landen Road
And one from Garryowen

Memory of an Old Seadog
by
Claire Galligan

Building boats daily to produce the perfect miniature replica of the Hud, H.M.S Britannica and the Sovereign of the Seas keeps me alert and alive. This workshop on wooden boat building organised by the Simon Community offers us a respite from the flat pavements, drizzling rain, and the unkind wind which wraps itself around us, and is as restless as a stormy sea in the height of Winter.

Building my boats takes me back to memories of my life in the British Navy. I miss the structure, and the discipline now. I rose up through my diligence to structure. I learned my craft from the Masters at Harland and Woolf shipyard in Belfast.

Ah those were the days when my hands were as steady as the prow of a large liner cutting a pathway like a sharp knife through a calm sea. But those hands succumbed to the unsteadiness of Alcohol. When I worked, I always protected my eyes with goggles from the flints of steel which hopped off the metal surface of the rolled steel joist that I was working on. However, one day, I was suffering from a particularly nasty hangover, and I was irritated by my goggles'. *It's only a short piece of steel, so I'll risk it'.* Foolishly, I believed that I was invincible in those days and- that I would have a job for life-until that morning when an acetenyl blast scarred my unprotected left eye. It was their excuse to let me go- and they did.

It wasn't the blast of acetenyl more the blast of alcohol which quenched my thirst for company in those days in Belfast. As long as I had a drink, I didn't need company. I was a Catholic, a token Catholic, so it was hard for me to be accepted; most of the men were Protestant. I was excluded even though my skills were respected, and the men sought out my company- only when a particularly difficult plan of a ship foxed their abilities. I must admit that I was attracted to the idea of being needed. Now I am not needed anymore and I don't need anything from anyone- just two Aldi shopping bags filled with bread and milk, and a bed for the night at this Simon hostel. I have realised that what I need most now, is spiritual sustenance. The pleasure that I get from carving wood, sewing sails, painting the prow, is like finding a lost treasure chest in the depth of my soul.

My boats will never sail, never be launched by her majesty the Queen, never carry soldiers to fight for some cause- but they are my children born and bred in this homeless hostel. I give them life; I shape their ebony souls; I don't have any family to bequeath my treasures to- but they will live, long after I have paid the Ferryman to take me to the afterlife.

When people read the inscription 'Happy but Scrappy' underneath my boat, in the exhibition of artistic projects organised by the Simon Community- I hope that I will

live in someone's memory, and they will recognise that I
once had a talent.

Won't Apologise
by
Richard O'Shea

I won't apologise, for anything I do
Just like the government's lies
That they feed to you
We mourn, dead presidents
But nobody cares about the residents that live in a house
that is ready to fall
Is that all
Is that all

We need someone, like Robin Hood
Who, slays the evil, helps the good
Probably be arrested, molested, detested

Change
The world, doesn't stop, if you might fail
Are in jail or impaled
On a spike of a nail
That is stuck in your hand
From the cross that you bear, that was not in your plan

You might be tempted, to rent it and then spend it
With rent prices rising, government not giving a toss
Sell it with luxurious view,
You can see from the cross

We need to protest, be devoted,
Not bloated
With shit that we read on face book and twitter

Get more educational knowledge, in a public shitter

Get a truck, get a crane,
To pry open your eyes
Then a power washer to clean away
The scum and the lies
Remember do it, before your dead,
If you don't bother, that stale shit gets stuck in your head
Ever notice, you've been living a lie
If you did
Then all you would want to do is cry or sigh or die or buy
A new life for yourself, where you're not gathering dust, while you sit on the shelf
Waiting for it all to change by someone else

Change
The world, doesn't stop, if you might fail
Are in jail or impaled
On a spike of a nail
Already in your hand
From the cross that you bear that was not in your plan

Realise
by
Richard O'Shea

I'm slowly starting to realise, that I got to utilise
Anything that suppresses me, helps me rise above
Like the things that drags me under, tears my confidence
asunder but I'm not the only person here
So enough about me

Let's talk about the homeless, on the verge of constant
suicide,
The government doesn't realise or maybe just close their
eyes
Well they definitely, don't provide
Whoever gets the powers, who gives a fuck about the
hours?
Living on the street, to try to make ends meet
Yes we got a problem, but it's getting so much better
Yes, it's great to sleep outside, with the country getting
wetter
Wouldn't you contemplate suicide, to try to fucking hide?
The fact the government failed you, which is tearing up
your pride
He used to have life; he used to have a wife, now he's
got a concrete mattress that cuts him like a knife
Of course, he didn't plan it, just turned out that way
I failed; I failed, it's all I got to say
Well he's not the person whom, life hasn't gone to plan
Who jumped from a bad situation, from the fire place to
the burning pan.

We've got, to have a better understanding, in a world so demanding

Try not lose sight, in a day to day world war personal fight

With yourself, your friend, any fucker till the bitter end,

Let's not pretend, wrong message not to send

Let's try to be a pacifist, who still stands strong and hold up their fist

Who'd never ever get angry but for the right reason, would be pissed

For the things we cannot swallow, because we know there just not right,

So let's join the right people, right cause, right direction, right correction, right connection,

 Right Perfection

And make, this world shine bright

Come on guys

Let's make it fucking happen

Or I'm gonna keep rapping

Slapping, grapping, flapping, mapping

A better path

Josh
by
Joanne Cullivan

Josh Monroe lay across the wooden bench in the Garda station, his clothes still damp from wandering around on a wet day in the city. He knew it would be a while before the social workers arrived, as the guards informed him they were placing other young people in hostels. He tried to fall asleep, but the bustle of people in and out of the Garda station kept him from much needed rest.

It was 12.40 a.m. when the social workers finally arrived. Josh was looking forward to warm food and a bed for the night, as well as freshly laundered clothes in the morning.

After he was admitted into the hostel by social care staff, Josh took himself off to the kitchen to get himself something to eat. Afterwards, he watched some telly and had a go on the playstation, with some of the other young people, before heading to bed. Some of the young people he knew from being on the streets, others he didn't, which meant they were probably new to homelessness.

In his bedroom for the night, Josh turned on the radio, to try and distract himself from the thoughts in his head. He was thinking about the last time he saw his dad. It was almost six years ago, on his twelfth birthday. He remembered how his dad had a big row with his mum that day. He didn't know what it was about, but he did remember the blazing rows between them, when he was younger. His dad drank a lot. He left the house that day and never returned. Josh got the odd birthday card from him now and again, but that was about it. He turned up the radio and listened to Adrian Kennedy and Jeremy Dixon debate the hot topic of the night. Eventually, he fell asleep.

The following morning arrived. Josh pushed his cornflakes from one side of the bowl to the other with his spoon, not really paying attention to the conversations between the other young people. He was anxious about the day and night ahead.

"Not hungry today, Josh," one of the care staff asked, noticing.

"Nah," he replied, "I'll get something later on in town."

"We might see you again tonight, or in a few days?"

"Not me. I'm eighteen today. I'll have to go to adult services from now on."

"Gosh, Josh, sorry, I didn't realise. Happy Birthday. I hope you get a bed later. Make sure you ring in early. Best of luck."

"Yeah...eh...thanks!"

It was 10a.m when Josh left the hostel. He was still tired, but there was no point in trying to sleep during the day, with the various city sounds. Instead, he sat outside the bus station and begged for a while. At least it was a dry day and he wouldn't get wet again.

He hoped to make enough money to get himself a sandwich and a hot drink. Sometimes, a kind person passing would buy these for him, but that was a rare occurrence and certainly not a daily one. Most times, he found people didn't even look at him. It was like he was invisible to the world. It's not as if he didn't have dreams, just like everyone else. He hoped to work in construction someday. He didn't know how he would go about this, but he would certainly try.

He was offered jobs on the streets, pedalling drugs. He knew it was a lucrative one, but one he was not happy to do. He never dabbled in drugs, although the occasion had presented itself, more than once. He had seen too many of his friends on the streets pass away from drug overdoses. Although Josh had been homeless for three years, he hoped that someday he would get out of it. The guards came and he was asked to move on. They spot-searched him for drugs. They did both a lot.

Later, Josh, rang the emergency phone number to get a bed. They told him that all the beds were full for the night. He was forced to sleep on the streets. It wasn't his first time, however. It was a very hard life for him. He had been on the streets since he left his Mum's house, at the age of fifteen. He'd had a massive row with her, which resulted in him throwing things, narrowly missing his Mum in the process. Josh got angry sometimes. He didn't understand why. He just knew that he couldn't control it. She asked him to leave that day, or she would call the guards. So he left that day and never returned.

He went to a busy bridge in the city and sat there for a while, until some workers from a homeless charity came along and offered him some food and a hot drink. Afterwards he went to where he had hidden his sleeping bag from two nights previous, hoping it was still there. Thankfully it was, so he bedded down for the night behind a large building in the city centre. It was well known by the homeless that there were pipes running underneath the ground at the back of the building, which provided a little heat. The city was quieter now, so he hoped sleep would come quickly. It was a bitter cold night. Josh wished for one thing, that he would wake up tomorrow.

The invisible house
by
Violeta Geraghty

My house is invisible
The street is my house
My home is the street
And when it rains I wish I had a house
Especially when it rains
Because I can go home and keep myself dry
And look out the window at the rain.

Wishes
by
By R.G. Bighiu

I had wishes like dreams
Like fishes that swam in seams of desires...
They evaporated in wishes
Like dreams that fight nightmares.

I am frightened, it stinks!
My life is scribbled in rotten ink.
I tried not to smear the edges.
But every line holds me in a prison.

I had dreams, they whispered paths of living.
Now I race this maze in tune with screams of fears.
Still, I misplace my wishes in hidings
Cause I fear the instant I become wish-less.

Hope, my guardian or my prisoner?
In this dichotomy of lies
I arise as a philosopher of hell.
Unwell, and blinded my tears hold hope!

So once again, I have wishes
Like dreams that fight nightmares.
I let myself hold my desires close,
So, every line becomes a song,
Of better path to a lived-up life.

Liffey bridge
by
Catriona Murphy

Jam-pressed
In the Good 'Aul Times
You beamed at me
And said
'Chocolate on your face love!'
Funny
How yis talk to anyone.

Disarmed
By your unguardedness
Only happy soul I saw
In the city that day.

You're pockets
Of humanity
Scattered
Across Dublin one
Life smeared on your faces -
Gaunt
Hopeful
Lost
Nowhere
Everywhere.

Unbeknownst you're sparkling
Our hope
Balanced gently
Feathering

Precariously
On your torn shoulders.

A moonbeam path
Of God's love
Unfolds before
Your veteran feet
A glowing trail
Follows yis everywhere.

Brasilia Café
by
Sinéad MacDevitt

When ejected from my slumber
from the bus too soon each Monday,
I paused at Brasilia's breast
of brown toast and poached eggs

Until the morning of the twenty-sixth,
the waitress made an announcement.
No ceremony after thirty-five years.
After all, it was Monday morning.

To say goodbye and catch the year:
the same year that I started to wean
towards work, was all over in a flash
as I left to find another breast.

When I returned from *The Wooden Whisk*,
chairs were stacked and shutters down.
No shop front left, only the logo to photograph
before all would become shadowed by a chain.

A Walk and Talk in California Hills Park, Ballyfermot
by
Sinéad MacDevitt

A cluster of people assembled in the park on that chilly morning on 12th April 2019. The population ranged from children in school uniforms to senior citizens. Heads magnetised towards a lady holding a microphone and clothed in a long brown coat. Éanna Ní Lamhna's energetic voice welcomed us to the lungs of Ballyfermot: the trees.

She introduced us to the herring gulls who make their living in the city. In the morning only the boy birds sing, much to the amusement of the third and fourth class boys in the blue school uniform. The male birds are issuing war cries because they are claiming territory but one thing that the male birds can't do is lay eggs. So they need a woman. This was followed by cheers from the schoolgirls.

Éanna confessed because she does more talking than walking, we will be walking fast. We hitched up our step and bustled our way along the grass towards the tree which was alleged to "have a very bad smell", the Elder tree. The reason why it has a bad smell is because the elder tree was supposed to have been cursed. It was cursed because this was the tree where Judas was supposed to have hanged himself. And God said to the tree "you will be cursed and you will never be able to have anyone hanging themselves on you again". And the timber of the elder tree is very weak and is all hollow inside. So the timber is not strong enough to bear anyone's weight. Apparently, if you hit someone with a bit of an elder, they won't grow any bigger. (Not that she was going to). If you make a boat out of it, it will sink and anyone will drown. If you make a cradle out of it, the baby will die. However, if you gather the elderflowers and put them in water and sugar for a fortnight, you will have the most beautiful champagne. In the autumn time, the elder tree grows berries, which are very good for the birds. But they won't kill us, they are just a bit sour. The good news is that the tree doesn't grow in the holy land. She rounded off the topic by saying "why would one spoil a good story with facts."A chorus of laughter rose.

Underneath the elder tree, there are wild flowers as planned by Dublin City Council. The reason for the wild flowers is to give the insects the opportunity for them to pollinate. Among the flowers of various colours, are the yellow flowers called dandelions. We learned how the dandelion was used as a cure for dropsy during the time there were no doctors so cures came from plants. So if one's leg swelled which was a sign of dropsy, it was recommended that one would eat twenty five dandelion leaves. The Irish word for dandelion is the bitter herb, *Caisearbhán*.The French word for dandelion, is pissenlit, or to make it clearer "piss on lee", which set the children into a fit of laughter.

After another stroll through the grass, she pointed to the trees with green and orange dots growing on the bark:

lichens. Lichens are small plants. It was declared that lichens only grow where the air quality is good. Lichens don't have roots. They get their nourishment from the air. In the past there were no lichens on the trees because of the pollution. Thanks to Mary Harney bringing in the Clean Air Act in 1990. So Éanna said: "if there are lichens on the trees, we can all hyperventilate".

As the crowd pulsed forward, the cacophony of chatter was punctuated by the clicking of phones and cameras.

On we surged towards a large shrub with flowers, another native Irish tree, known as the sweet-smelling tree: the Hawthorn tree. Whitethorn in the summer and Hawthorn in the Autumn. In the Autumn, there are red berries on the hawthorn tree known as haws. It was considered long ago to smell like a dead body. However, it was stated in the past that the hawthorn was supposed to bring bad luck to houses. She entertained us with the story about the preservation of the hawthorn tree in Munster, if we believe in fairies. Approximately twenty years ago, there was a bypass being built in Ennis in County Clare. A hawthorn tree was going to be cut down. According to a myth, the fairies of Munster used to dance around the tree. A man was going to cut down the tree but the saw wouldn't work. He travelled back to get a heavy chainsaw machine. However, on his return before he reached the tree, his car crashed. So the tree remained intact, thanks to the fairies. This was echoed by nods, grins and thumbs up not only from the children but from the adults.

We paraded onwards until the group formed a cluster towards one of the tallest trees with flat broad leaves. This tree was associated with Synge's phrase, "as naked as an ash tree in the moon of May". A great way of remembering what an Ash tree looks like.

We followed her towards the tree with last year's leaves still on them - the loopy leaves, which belonged to the Oak tree: the only trees with loopy trees which that form acorns. And the ash tree was very bare at this time. So the oak and ash are the last of the trees to get their leaves.

If you want to predict the weather for the summer, observe the oak and ash during the spring as per the instructions in this rhyme.

If the Oak comes out before the Ash,
there'll be a summer splash.
If the Ash comes out before the Oak,
there'll be a summer soak.

It looks like the loopy leaves were first to bud in the year 2019, as I don't recall using my umbrella very much during my summer holidays.

A few more yards onwards, we met the ladies of the woods: the elegant silver trees with small leaves. These Birch trees were surrounded by spring flowers, the bluebells.

We were confronted with a Tree of War. A tree with a red branch, a tree with flowers, the only tree with cones and a native Irish tree: the Alder tree.

Onwards we veered towards another Irish root tree, the Crab Apple tree with apples that come to fruition in Autumn. Well worth visiting California Hills Park in the Autumn.

Another giant plant with lovely white flowers and red berries that stood majestically was the Rowan tree. It is also known as Mountain Ash. According to a myth, if you plant the tree near your house, it keeps away the witches. If you plant it near a grave, it will keep the dead from rising.

After another brisk walk, a large plant with a spreading bushy habit framed our view: the Hazel tree known as the tree of wisdom. Several hazel trees grew on the banks of the River Boyne. According to the legend, the nuts fell into the river and were eaten by the Salmon of Knowledge.

We were shown another woodland growth, known as stickybacks, formally known as Cleavers or Robin-run-the-hedge. The purpose of the stickiness is to spread the seeds. That's how Velcro was invented, thanks to the stickyback.

In between the pauses of Éanna's delivery and the participants' one-liners, a trilling sound of a bird could be heard: the robin.

According to a recent survey, it proved that 40% of Irish kids never climbed trees. Years ago, climbing trees was a common hobby, so much so that apparently one parent said: "don't come in unless you're bleeding".

I dare say, why would we need to travel to California to climb their hills in order to see the world below, when we can go as far as Ballyfermot to see Dublin 10 spread out below the trees? Why would we need to plant imported trees when we have so many lovely Irish trees?

On the way back to the entrance, we heard a two-note sound: "teacher teacher" from the Great Tit. As we listened, it sounded like the pumping of a bicycle. Not necessarily a common sound in 2019, is it? Now with the purer air revealed by the lichens, cycling is a hobby well worth considering. Hence the constant need of trees to purify the atmosphere: the more trees, the more oxygen in the air.

Éanna not only left us with a feast of information but a feast of food and drink that can be foraged from California Hills Park.

Vacancy
by
Alan O'Farrell

The profane rites have been performed
and documented at the flat's door,
paper to prove the old tenants should now
be no more substantial than ghosts:
a spooked neighbour has said
they've not been seen since a loud row
suddenly fell silent months ago.
In the damp courtyard there is no noise for a moment
save for the bins where the wind is catching
the edges of cardboard boxes and flapping plastic.
We've lapsed into solemnity, despite ourselves.
Then the drill's motor roars, breaking our silent poise
Until it stops seconds later and the buckled lock
falls to the floor with a clunk and the door creaks open.
We enter with hesitant, lawful-minded caution,
Pushing against the weight of a pile of unread letters
As the long-inured locksmith loiters
Outside briefly, before departing unobtrusively.
Inside there is a stagnant smell of cold, dead air
from a toilet unflushed for months but
otherwise no bodies have been disturbed
except a pair of pigeons fluttering out
an open window.
Unused nappies, empty bottles and clothes
lie strewn about the rooms as food moulders
on plates: the fossil counterparts
of a home frozen at its end.

All present agree it could easily be worse,
but I'm shocked nonetheless: such fugitive lives
and sudden vanishings are miles
from my experience on the blunt, soft side of life.
We get to work tidying the detritus,
banishing the cold, hoping to dispel
The past and all its unsettled, unsettling signs.

Liberties Whiskey Fire
by
Derek Copley

One night I lay on the cold ground
not the first time nor the last
in a dark little corner in the Liberties
where I'd often take me rest
I'd a long oul day out begging
and not much left to show
after drinking my hard earnings
'round the streets of Pimlico

It was on a summer evening
but the wind it still blew cold
maybe it was the full day's drink in me
that made me feel so old
either way this life was far too hard
and I swore it was time to change
I'd head up to the nuns in the morning
my saviour to arrange

Now trying to find a bit of warmth
I huddled myself to sleep
and I tried to dream of a warm paradise
with blue skies running deep
right then I was sure I was dreaming
was I in heaven or was I in hell
cos molten lava surrounded me
but it was whiskey I could smell

Right before my very eyes

a fire lit up the sky
and I could hear the hellish clap of hooves
which did me terrify
to beat the devil I said a prayer
that I'd drink no more a drop
save me from this devilish place
and my devilish ways I'll stop

Well I don't know if my prayer it worked
or was it just God's funny way
but the clap of hooves turned out to be pigs
running from their sty
what made them bolt it did turn out
and the fire lighting up the sky
was a blaze down in the malt house
that sent whiskey flowing free

Now the whiskey burned like lava
as it flowed down Ardee Street
the pigs used their brains and got away
but they were all that did retreat
for instead of fleeing to safety
men and women gathered round
with what they could use even their own shoes
to scoop the whiskey off the ground

I'm telling you now it was quite the sight
A river of whiskey it was a first
and if it wasn't for the blessed prayer
I'd said I would've dived straight in head first
nevermind the fact that the fireman

Mr Ingram a rare breed you know
he lay down a ton of horse manure
to halt the whiskey's flow

Now you mightn't believe me temptation
and sure the perils of fire are well known
but try think of the situation
in the Liberties on the 18th of June
for despite the flames and the danger
thirteen people ended up dead
not from burns or smoke inhalation
it was drinking hot whiskey instead

Well I tell you this for nothing
a penance that night I served
and there's ne'er a priest nor a nun
say it wasn't well deserved
for it got me back to religion
and I pray now every night
and I won't take a drink no more til I see
the whiskey flow down Ardee Street

*This song can be listened to on Bandcamp under the
name Derek Copley.

This Is No Home
by
Derek Copley

As I lie here
My body's black and blue
And my heart's as cold as the stones on the wall
That keep us in here like prisoners
for doing nothing at all
Never to go home for the crimes they tell us that we
have done
Charged as a baby and taken away to the Brothers and
the Nuns

Chorus:
And they teach us about heaven
but they beat us into hell
They smile through our tears
Little children left in fear
This is no home

What is a child
As far as I know it's a little boy or girl who is forced to
go
To the laundry house or make the rosary beads for the
Holy Joes
And you're not allowed laugh or jump around and sing
kids' songs
So you have to get back to work
Or you'll be sorry that you were born

As I'm older now
I lay here and I'm too sore to dream that this life can change
Is it wrong of me to want to go and to get my revenge
For the life I was forced to live in place of what I was refused
By the bastards who made me believe that my beatings were well deserved

When children cry
their mothers and their fathers should be able to come running
and ask them why
To rub their knees and dry their eyes and kiss their child
But the children of the institutes could never know such care
Their mother's embrace is replaced by the cold hard bitin stare

In their own right minds
Nobody would say a child deserved to be abused
But nobody knew or would listen to the cries from the institutes
Now the blood drips slowly down through our society
And the stains of the past must never be left to wash away
Lest we forget the suffering which is still going on today

*This song can be listened to on Bandcamp under the name Derek Copley.

Morning Ramble ('round Ballyer)
by
Derek Copley

Cobwebs glisten call another morning
Footsteps fall to wake the dreaming dew
Birds and builders singing songs together
Flying now the day has just begun

Hear the hedgerow foragers in feeding
Chirping cries a young pup on the prowl
Blue skies tempt the footpath to grow longer
Breath of frosty air clears the head

Distant sounds of trucks and trailers shaking
Car horns sound up on the valley high
I could go on walking here forever
Whistling with the builders, birds and breeze

Sometimes I think about a time before me
of druids, gaels and ceremonies here
the embers of a firepit then reminds me
the empty cans the ritual of youth

Nighttime comes and dreams I hope are waiting
Helping these good days to carry on
Heavy clouds come to cast dark evening shadows
When they pass I'll rest among the stars

*This song can be listened to on Bandcamp under the
name Derek Copley.

The Things He Didn't Carry
by
Joseph Plowman

"Have you any jeans?" he said.
"No," I said. "Just chocolate, food and soap."
He lay on the verge.

There was more in the bag,
But not enough.
He took it,
Warmly,
Despite sleeping rough.
His jeans tied with felt
Round his shivering waist.
This Fair City.

Did he sense my shame?
Did he feel how tied I felt,
Like his jeans?
The things he didn't carry;
Their weight on my shoulders.

I see a snail
Moving in the grass.
The dignity of a snail.
The justice of a snail.
Carrying not a bag,
But a home.

Invisible
by
Chris Percival

Her name is Faye, a 30-year-old, from Dublin. This is her story. Although this story is fictitious, many of the themes explored represent a realistic portrayal of what some homeless women such as Faye have experienced. Faye was sexually abused when she was a child. She now has three children who are in the care of the state. One morning, Faye awoke to find her husband John dead, beside her in their bed. John had kissed his three children goodnight, like he did most nights. He fell asleep and never woke up. John died from Sudden Arrhythmic Death Syndrome (SADS). Faye, John and their three children, Erica 10, Jane 7, and Paul 4, appeared to live a perfectly normal life. Both Faye and John worked in professional jobs. Faye was a Bank Manager and John worked in the Financial Services sector. Faye had worked hard since joining the Bank, working in the Customer Service front desk in her local branch.

After her husband's death, Faye found herself trying to come to terms and cope with the reality of the situation she now found herself in. Dealing with John's death was extremely difficult for her. She had lost the father to her children, the love of her life and her soul mate. Faye found herself grieving silently, trying to hide her emotions from the children. At the same time needing to be so strong for them. Feeling overwhelmed with the situation, Faye presented to her family Doctor. For her low mood, she was prescribed anti-depressants, for the anxiety she was experiencing, she was prescribed a sedative and for her sleepless nights, she was prescribed a sleeping tablet. Fay at some point during this tumultuous period turned to illegal drugs to help her cope. It started out with a little cocaine in the morning to get her through the day. This was further compounded when she began abusing the medication her Doctor had prescribed her, mixing it with alcohol. And so, this cycle continued for some time, Faye would take Cocaine and prescribed medication during the day followed by sleeping tablets and some alcohol at night.

Mourning the loss of a loved one is exceedingly difficult to say the least. For Faye, cracks began to appear in her everyday life. She was so consumed by her need to cope with the demands of being a strong mother to her children, she forgot to look after herself. The reality for her though, was that she neglected to care for her, the grieving spouse. Not just Faye, the mother. There were many days when she couldn't face getting out of bed, washing herself, or even getting dressed. The very thought of trying to get through another day at times seemed too much for her. As the cracks appeared, Faye found herself alone with no support network around her.

Ten years ago, when Faye was around 20 years old, her relationship with her family broke down. After her dad's death, she disclosed to her mother and three siblings that her Uncle, on her dads' side of the family, had sexually abused her when she was just 7 years old, until she turned 12. This revelation by Faye to her family was rebuffed. Her mother Mary was a conservative woman, deeply religious and was a devout Catholic. Sadly, her mother Mary and her siblings refused to believe her. Instead forcing Faye to keep quiet about the abuse, to avoid shaming the family. The trauma that she experienced in her childhood would follow her throughout her life into adulthood.

Despite her strength and courage, Faye's adverse childhood experiences were merely pushed down somewhere deep inside her. That was until she found her husband John dead. His death acted as a volcanic eruption for her. All the trauma in her life began pouring out. That tragic morning something inside Faye was shattered. There were days when she would just stay in bed, wrapping herself in John's clothes, trying to hold on to the scent from each piece of clothing. This she found, would bring her close to him again, even for just a moment. Eventually the smells, that Faye found so much comfort in began to fade, until one day she could no longer smell John's scent anymore.

Things were beginning to unravel at home. The children noticed their mum was always crying, in bed or drinking. Erica, the eldest, found herself getting her sister Jane and brother Paul ready for school every morning and making their breakfast. Their mum frequently hungover and groggy from the alcohol and sleeping tablets the night before began to neglect the children's needs. The children would often have no dinner or supper and would go to bed hungry. They also began to be absent from school frequently. Eventually there was a Social

Worker appointed to work with the family after a referral from the children's school. It became clear to the Social Worker, that Faye's life had spiralled out of control. Her past trauma, her inability to cope with her husband's tragic death, along with her addiction issues were the core reasons why her life had come to this point. Despite the efforts of the Social Worker to provide the proper supports for Faye and her family, an intervention came too late.

At 2am on a Saturday night, Paul was found wondering the streets. The 4-year-old had wondered out onto the street when his mum had gone outside, leaving the front door open. Faye had arranged to meet a local drug dealer to buy some tablets. She was now abusing cocaine, sedatives, sleeping tablets and alcohol. As she haggled with the drug dealer, Paul managed to slip by her unnoticed. Faye soon after, passed out from the alcohol and tablets she had taken, oblivious her son was in grievous danger. Paul was found by a couple, who were returning from a night out in the City. He was lost, cold and scared when they found him. Luckily, Paul was unharmed, and the nice couple looked after him until help arrived. The children were subsequently taken into care and placed in foster homes. Sadly, for the children they were split up and placed in separate foster homes.

For Faye, her situation was perilous. Now embroiled in addiction, she lost her job working in the Bank. Unable to keep up with the mortgage payments, she lost her home and found herself homeless. Faye spent her first night homeless, lying beside John's gravestone. Sadly, for her, she would have many nights like this. She would score some drugs, drink alcohol, and fall asleep by his grave. There was a part of her wishing that she would fall asleep and never wake up.

Afraid to stay in homeless hostels, Faye slept on the streets for several months. During this time things were extremely challenging for her. She had lost everything. Riddled with the guilt of losing her children, she hated herself. She had lost her sense of self and continued a downward spiral. In her own mind, Faye knew she was moving further away from her children and the life she had with them. Yet she felt powerless to turn things around. Consumed with guilt, Faye tried heroin for the first time. She had been offered it by a girl she had met on the streets. Faye had got to know Monica as they had slept in the same alleyway. This was the first time Faye would experience an overdose. A few hours later, she found herself in a hospital. She had been administered several doses of Naloxone by the paramedics who found her unresponsive.

It had been months since she had seen her three children. Sleeping rough on the streets of Dublin, Faye felt invisible. She quickly learned that to survive the daily rat race, she had to be resourceful. She also learned she needed to be tough to survive on Dublin's streets. Faye soon would learn not all people were as nice to her as her friend Monica. Although Monica had been the one who gave her the heroin she would overdose on. She was a good friend to her. Monica had called the ambulance for Faye, instead of leaving her to die in a rotten alleyway. Monica had showed her the way things worked on the streets. Where to go for food, clothes, warmth, and shelter. Where it was safe to sleep at night and who it was safe to mingle with. Monica who was homeless for several years would later die on Dublin's streets from a heroin overdose.

On one night, a homeless outreach team came across Faye, she wasn't sleeping in her regular spot in the alleyway in town. She had decided to move after Monica had overdosed and died. She was now sleeping in a tent in the Phoenix Park. Here she felt safer. There was a storm due and Faye for the first time agreed to stay in emergency accommodation. She was grateful for the support the Outreach Team had given her. Faye's first night in the homeless hostel was not a positive experience. While she was asleep, all her belongings were robbed including the wedding ring John had given her. This further widened the gap that existed in her mind about staying in homeless accommodation. She returned to the streets the following day.

Faye was at rock bottom. She was now estranged from her children for almost a year and had not seen them since they were placed in foster care. To pay for her heroin addiction which had escalated, she engaged in prostitution. She now felt completely downtrodden and had no hopes of a positive future for herself. She could not bear to think of John and the three children. To repress her emotions, her thoughts, she turned to her new friend heroin. The heroin helped her numb the inextricable pain she had inside. When she would take it, she felt nothing, just a numbness. It was the gap in between her thoughts she needed to suppress. In that void Faye would hear her inner voice. The inner child, the adult and the critical parent would sometimes appear from the shadows of her thoughts. To suppress the ugliness of her reality, she found solace in heroin.

Isolated from her family, friends, and her children. Faye felt a loneliness, an emptiness, that only a mother could feel. She thought about the kids and John all the time. She struggled to come to terms that John was gone, that he was dead. Erica, Jane, and Paul were in foster care, this burden played on Faye's mind. She would sometimes go over and over in her head asking herself, how did I end up like this? Why did John have to die? Why could I not cope when he died? Why did I not try to reach out for more support? Why did I turn to drugs? Although Faye had some answers to these questions, her solution she felt, was always to turn to heroin.

Heroin would be Faye's nemesis. Her addiction now had control over her. It was a chaotic affair between them. Her addiction and her use of heroin was highly regulated. Faye knew how long she would last before needing another fix. If she didn't get it, she would soon begin to feel sick and get withdrawal symptoms. As the clasp of heroin addiction consumed her. Fay was forced to engage in prostitution to pay for her drugs. This would sometimes place her in dangerous situations. Although she had regular punters, men she knew to see and tended to meet the same punters because she felt safer doing this. One night when she met a regular punter, he brought her to an apartment, Faye was okay with this and she felt safe with her decision. The situation, however, became more perilous when the punter decided to invite his friends to the apartment unknown to her. Faye unsure what to do, decided to stay. She felt she had no choice. There was a lot of drugs used by the punter and his friends. Things quickly escalated and soon turned ugly. Faye was gang raped in the apartment by the punter and his three friends. When her ordeal was over, she gathered her belongings and quickly left the apartment. She was in a state of shock. Too scared, she decided not to tell anyone. Faye felt because she was engaging in prostitution, no one would believe her, and no one would care. She never told a soul what had happened her that night. She eventually made her way back to her tent in the Phoenix Park. Traumatised from what had happened, she injected heroin and passed out. The next day Faye was still upset and scared after what had happened. She decided to see a doctor in a drop-in clinic and received the morning after pill. She didn't tell the Doctor what happened to her the night before.

The gang rape was too much for Faye. She blamed herself for putting herself in the situation. She felt ashamed about what had happened. It was a bridge too far for her. Too big of a burden for her to hold and it pushed her over the edge. Three days after the incident, she committed suicide. Faye was found by an early morning jogger. She had hung herself from a tree in the Phoenix Park. There was no headline in the newspapers, there was no mention at all. There was no mention of Faye's suicide on the news. It was like it never happened. Ironically if she had been in a road traffic accident it would have been noted in the media. Faye had become invisible in life, on the streets of Dublin and invisible in death. She became a number, just another statistic, where a homeless person had died on the streets of Ireland's capital.

One only had to merely scratch the surface of Faye's life to see the open wounds of her childhood trauma. A childhood trauma never acknowledged, never dealt with, just buried. Buried so deep in a vault of her subconscious mind. It was untouchable. That is, until that fateful morning when she discovered John, her husband, her best friend, her soul mate, dead. This was the catalyst that sparked an outpouring of unresolved trauma for Faye. A tragic event she would never recover from. That would lead her down a pathway of addiction, poverty, prostitution, homelessness, and suicide. Faye and John's three children, Erica, Jane, and Paul had now lost both their parents in the space of a year. Their world had been turned upside-down. They are also the victims in this story. They will spend the remainder of their young lives in a foster care setting. They will never be able to hug their parents or tell them how much they love them. They will never be able to kiss their mum and dad goodnight. They will have to somehow move forward with their lives without their parents. How could it have come to this? Where did it all go wrong for Faye? What caused her to begin abusing drugs? Why did she decide to end her life? When the children were faced with losing both their parents, what impact did this have on them and on the remainder of their lives?

In tragic cases like Faye and her family, so many questions are asked, but few answers provided. This story is a heart-breaking one. It is a story that is not uncommon in Ireland in 2021. There are so many individuals and families struck by tragedy, who end up in situations like Faye and her family. Many others find themselves in difficult circumstances due to socio-economic factors such as poverty or a lack of housing options due to the current housing crisis that Ireland is facing at present. Many are living in cramped and overcrowded tenancies. Evictions of tenants by Landlords remains an ongoing issue.

For Faye, perhaps her past trauma profoundly affected her. Would things have turned out differently if she had been believed and supported by her family? With adequate supports provided for her, would this have prevented her tragic death? The simple answer is, we will never know. Trauma passes from one generation to the next. There are many children like Faye's, in Ireland today that have been affected by their parent's trauma. Faye may not have had the childhood supports, but perhaps by using a Trauma Informed Care approach, the children of this country can have a more positive outcome.

This story is dedicated to all the homeless people I have worked with over the past thirteen years. Your strength and courage to survive and flourish each day has inspired me. You've inspired me to be a better worker and a better person. Despite the outrageous acts of cruelty that has been placed upon you, you always glowed like that of a shining star in the night sky. For those like Faye, who could not bear to take another blow, from a society that did not see you, let me say this, you are not invisible, we see you. Never give up hope. There is always something worth holding on for. You are all my heroes.

Survive and Thrive
by
Chris Percival

They say, you were abused
They say, you are damaged
They even say you are mad.

I say, you are a survivor
I say, you are perfect
I say, you are indifferent.

They say, you are abusive
They say, you are aggressive
They say you are needy.

I say, you are respectful
I say, you are peaceful
And you have been hurt.

They said you were nothing
I say, you are everything.
They don't see you, yet they judge you
I see you. I see you.

They say you will die
I say, you will live.
For inside you, there is a spirit, that will never die.
A spirit that will survive and thrive.

Aegis
by
Brendan Canning

If we had Zeus's aegis, would it be sufficient
In the battle against the global scourge
The worldly virus that shows no quarter
Yes, we have the mask and the visor
But which is more efficacious
The face covering vis a vis the visor
For an answer, we consult
doctors, professors, scientists
Then Nphet will meet with government
And our Taoiseach will address the Irish tribe.

Let Them Eat Grass
by
Erinna Behal

115 people dead
One and a half grand to rent a shed
6,700 without their own bed
Ah yeah, but sure at least they haven't fled
From wars and wars and rumours of wars
That's why they're dead, of course, of course
They're nothing at all but ne'er-do-wells
You can't help those who won't help themselves

No room at the Inn, no room at the Manger
Go walk the streets, go stay out of danger
The bright shiny future of Coliving Slums
The doors thrown open for Vulture Funds
And the Love One Anothers as I have Loved Youse
Are all sitting pretty in neat little pews

Junkies, howayas, bums and scum
Someone's daughter, someone's son
The abused child, the autistic one
Someone to take turns pissing on
From Rugby bros in Mercs and Porsches
To Welfare Inspectors in homeless services
All take their aim and piss in the face
Of the lost lonely child of the human race.

Thieves in the Temple Bar (Fleet Street)
by
Joseph Anthony O'Connor

Formerly the seventy-eight,
Seventy-eight A and B, and seventy-nine
Bus terminus to and from Ballyfermot,
I'd have never, ever thought, back in that time,

Happily ensconced with a drunken bus driver and
conductor
In between shifts,
In 'The Auld Dubliner',
Suppin' pints with King's crisps,

That there'd be a bouncer on the door one day,
More than likely not a native,
Who'd ask: *Have you had a drink already today?*
And—as if I'd ever be so uncreative

To pretend otherwise to gain entry
To a bar that already bears the name
Of my home town identity,
In the heart of my own city; the same

Auld bar I left many's a time with the aforesaid drunken
bus driver,
Who then drove me home, along with the bus load,
Back in the day when you could get flutered on a fiver—
'Twould be hard to answer and not explode!

Their pints being so dear now, I'd have nowt to offer but
this parting quip:
Jesus, if only I could have me a whip.

My Time in England (1980's)
by
Joseph Anthony O'Connor

It took no time to be made aware dat my th's lacked
pronunciation,
And, quite shockingly, of my race's supposed lack of
intellect;
And of the overall perception of us in that society's
imagination
As inferior (unless, for very different reasons, if one was
an elusive terrorist suspect)

No matter that I quoted Kavanagh, or Yeats, or the
witticisms of Wilde;
Or informed that Joyce had turned their language inside
out;
The trump card to cutting off any debate whenever
foiled
Revealed the Empire mentality still very much held its
clout.

Very funny people, though, wielding a great sense of
humour, therewith
Having great ability to laugh at themselves amongst
each other.
But, I never heard a joke begin "Have you heard about
the Englishman", pith.
'Twas not for the likes of us to jeer our betters.

Waiting for the Curer
by
Joseph Anthony O'Connor

(Main road, Ballyfermot, of a Sunday Morning)

Old men in big coats wait peevishly
Outside Downey's Lounge Bar
To get in ahead of opening time, ripe and ready
For the curer.

"Der's matches in deh Lawns later,
Cherryer and Ballyer United". Small-talk
Between drags. "Tap a bit harder
On dat winda, will ya horse?!"

Staid mass-goers stride by with an air.
Who'll be saved first?
My money is on Saint Bernard the barman over prayer,
Despite the disparity of the thirst.

Homlessness Means Helplessness
by
Mary Oyediran

"Are you alright back there?" Ade whispered trying not to wake baby Michael.

"Yes Mum" came a whimper from Debra.

She cast her motherly eyes upon them, Josh and Joyce slept sound. Debra was searching frantically for her torchlight to read her book.

"Hey you can finish that chapter tomorrow" she mused at her teenage bookworm.

"Oh Mum, I am nearly done!" Debra retorted.

Her husband Deji chipped in, staring ahead as he drove his little flock home.

"It has been a very long day. Lay your head down until we get home."

"Yes Daddy!" She admired her husband for his deep voice of wisdom, the children rarely argued with him.

"Nearly 10.30pm, it is so late." Mum whispered to her husband.

"It was a good revival, the Evangelist was inspiring, nobody wanted to go home." in a soft voice. "We'll be home by 11.00pm. No traffic tonight!" He drove smoothly and cautiously.

She looked at him fondly, recalling the days of his youthful exuberance before the children filled the car, he would speed down the expressway, her heart pounding in her mouth as she held her seat tight for dear life.

After the birth of his daughters he drove like a pensioner. She became mighty proud of him. She never teased him about it. She just respected his transformation to a family man.

Perfect timing, they arrived at the precisely at 11.00pm.

In his gentle deep voice, he took the roll call, "Joyce, Debra, Joshua, Michael, we are home " A chorus from the back of the car " Yes Daddy!" It worked every time. Their father's voice was a symphony in their ears. He was mighty proud of his children.

As he turned to enter the drive way, the gigantic iron gate was padlocked. That was unusual, these gates are never locked until all the cars were neatly parked in the driveway. He didn't press the horn, he didn't want to awaken the neighbours.

He came out the car to speak to the security man guarding the gates.

"Please open the gate!"

"No Oga! Today not open gate!" he answered looking down.

"Why?"

"Madame said no!", he replied. He was polite yet firm. Slowly her Deji returned, opened the car! "Your mother said they should not let us in."

"What? When?", trying to control her voice.

She deposited the baby gentle into her husband' s arm trying not to wake him. Smiling sweetly as she approached the security man.

He repeated his story. Madame said No!"

Then the balcony door flung open, it was her mother.

"Mummy is everything alright?" Looking up at her mother's morbid countenance.

"I want you to leave this house with your family tonight!"

"You will never sleep here again! Go and find your new home!" She yelled roaring like a lioness hungry for food.

Ade couldn't understand! They had no argument. In disbelief she called for her father. He came down to meet her. He was very calm looking nervous.

"Your mother is extremely upset, please go."

"Where to? Where should we go Daddy?"

They offered us a home in Lagos. Now, they are exercising their rights to take it back! Her father was torn between his beloved wife and his daughter.

Ade's husband beckoned to her. She returned to the car. Lucky for her Michael was still sleeping. The other children were wide awake, their eyes shone like stars. Their ears sharp as a razor, they soaked in their grandmother's words like a sponge. Her motherly instinct to love and protect them failed. it was too late!

They heard her as she spewed her emotions, rejecting her grandchildren too.

She sat in the car, as the baby was placed in her arms again. Her husband reversed the car! For the next 10 minutes the car was engulfed by a peaceful silence. Now the hunt for accommodation for the night. It was 11.30pm! They stopped in every motel. There was no room for a family of six. "No room at the inn" trying to humour the children. The truth is that Lagos motels were not designed for families. They specialised in other businesses. Families live in homes. The managers were kind but unapologetic reminding them that the motels couldn't accommodate children!

After hours of searching and no result.

Her nerves were frazzled. The baby was soaked, he was uncomfortable. All children became restless and famished. Deji stopped for some Lagos street food available 24/7. The aroma of sizzling hot fried yams, beans cakes and peppered meat Suya, washed down with coke cola satisfied every delicate taste bud. This meal was scrumptious and filled the empty bellies. They gobbled every bite and managed to smile through it all. After their meal, the search for a place to lay their head continued.

Lagos was dangerous. Not safe! Nobody cares at this time of night! Everyone with a decent family was neatly tucked in bed in their houses. Too dangerous to be out so late. The truth is life is cheap in Lagos. The dark sky like a woolly blanket covered them as they drove slowly on lonesome roads. She sensed danger and fear gripped her from within.

Suddenly her husband made this shocking announcement

"I have the church keys, let's go to church and sleep."

It was a bright idea! She agreed with him wholeheartedly. He drove back to the church, the day was breaking not a wink. How helpless she felt. Nothing could have prepared her for this night! Betrayal of parents. Homelessness for the first time in her life. Deep shame wrapped itself around her smothering her.

Finally they arrived at the church. Her husband opened the gates, drove in meticulously and parked the car carefully. The children had been cooped like chickens in a cage. They stretched, flapping their wings, happy to return back to a familiar place. The church was good to us. Tonight she loved this building more than ever.

Earlier in the evening, the church was liberating souls, full of joy, singing, dancing, laughter, swaying, preaching and prophecies. What a wonderful atmosphere they embraced! So much victory!

How did such a beautiful day end like this? This was the beginning of their homeless adventure. Tonight the church was their home. She felt embarrassed but thankful.

She always kept blankets in the car for long drives, these will keep the children warm for tonight. She changed Michael's diaper, he had a good skin - no rashes. He would get over this.

They prayed and thanked God for offering them a place to lay their head tonight. The real test for her was to forgive her mother. Right now, her heart was so broken, shattered into tiny fragments of glass. Will this pain heal? Her disgrace swelling in every joint of her bones.

"Never expected this, I am so sorry" she kept on whispering to her husband.

"Love everyone but trust God alone!" he whispered in her ears.

Then he embraced her in his arms. She held her tears for the sake of the children. She wanted to be strong but she was weakened by this rejection of her father and mother.

For the first time in her life she understood that homelessness was a state of helplessness.

The First Mod In Dublin
by
Camillus John

We all wondered why the section of skirting board gripped firmly in her left hand had a smattering of rusty nails hammered into and along its vintage far end. During a Heritage Week Walking Tour a few years ago, Dr. Ellen Rowley, architectural and cultural historian, took an original Herbert Simms skirting board, circa late 1940s Corporation Housing Estate, out of her haversack and began smish-smashing people over the head with it. Metaphorically speaking, of course.

You see, the rusty nails at the end draw blood and bring searing enlightenment almost instantaneously when shillelaghed over someone's head. Thereby, precipitating a quicker response and epiphany to her architectonic questions than otherwise would have been forthcoming organically. Time is of the essence on modernist walking tours.

'Hands up who's from Cabra, Crumlin, Ballyfermot, Henrietta House or Chancery House?' she asked. An eager fusillade of paws shot up.

'Where are you from?'
'Ballyfermot.'
'Who designed and built your house?'
'Don't know.'
'Who designed and built your house?'
'Don't know.'

The rusty-nailed skirting board came out of her handbag and over my head and across my face repeatedly until I screamed, 'Herbert Simms! Herbert Simms!' in a mouth-foaming fit of spewing sputum.

'Correctamundo,' she intoned from behind Samuel L. Jackson Pulp Fiction sunglasses.

Herbert Simms is the most important architect Ireland has ever seen. Or is likely to ever see. It's hard to disagree with such an opinion once privy to the brute facts. He architected the house I was brought up in – probably yours too on average if you're a Dub. Shut the door, he's now designing your window.

Herbert Simms was Housing Architect to Dublin Corporation from 1932 until 1948. Born in London and from a very modest background he studied architecture at Liverpool University with the aid of a scholarship earned as a result of his service in the First World War. He designed and built approximately 17,000 new dwellings in Dublin during that time. i.e. loads. His works encompassed striking flat blocks in the city centre (Henrietta House, Chancery House, Marrowbone Lane Flats) to herculean housing schemes of Byronic two-storey cottages in Crumlin, Cabra and Ballyfermot. They called this type of Corpo house, a cottage, back then for some unknown romantic reason to die for. Swoon.

This was at a time of mass state construction and provision of social housing. Looking back from the present era of chronic housing shortage and having seen the chances of any normal person being able to afford a home ever again going up in flames for generations to come, Herbert's oeuvre astounds and deranges the senses to the point of sentimentality. i.e. it's hard not to weep - or sooth yourself numb with water syringed directly from the river Lethe in mourning for the loss of a not-too-distant sort of prelapsarian Arcadia of astonishing housing plenitude we'll not see the likes of again. Metaphorically speaking like.

If you grew up in Cabra, Crumlin or Ballyfermot who've probably heard people say many, many times over that although the areas may have had their problems in the past, at least the houses were very well built. Solid. Of substance. And this is where Dr Ellen Rowley confirmed this widely-held belief by bringing her rusty-nailed skirting board of death out as proof of the black pudding. All of a sudden like. Unlike every Irish architect that came before and after him, Herbert, was a stickler for decent building standards. Like what Nye Bevan in England was doing when he wasn't busy creating the consummately-unimaginable-in-Ireland NHS. Most of Herbert's buildings are still standing to this day.

On one occasion when his superiors tried to obviate the requirement for skirting boards in one of his housing schemes, Herbie went bananas to such an extent that he threatened to chop off his left ear and post it to Archbishop McQuaid on a silver platter in protest. Metaphorically speaking, of course. They kept the skirting boards.

There was a strong flavour of a Van Gogh about his temperament which is quite apposite since his buildings display a huge Dutch influence by contemporaneous modernist apartment blocks by de Klerk in Amsterdam and J.P. Oud in Rotterdam. In evidence of this, he took part in a space-cake fuelled study trip to Amsterdam and Rotterdam in 1925 with his Dublin Corporation colleagues, and oh what a catalyst that turned out to be.

Therefore, the first mod in Dublin wasn't Paul Cleary from Ringsend band, The Blades, it was Herbert Simms, a sort of re-contextualised Paul Weller of Irish architects and as sharply dressed as the peacock suit facades of his city centre apartment blocks.

Vincent Van Gogh's work wasn't appreciated until after he passed away by shooting his brains out with a revolver and splattering them over his four living rooms walls. In a similar fashion, the way in which Herbert kissed the moon was all ravelled up with Archbishop McQuaid, Michael O'Brien (Dublin Corporation Town Planning Officer), housing schemes 'n' wheezes, pills, thrills and bellyaches.

During the 1930s, 1940s and beyond Irish Catholic "thinking" was that high rise flats were bad and two storey cottages (houses) were good like in George Orwell's two-legs-good-four-legs-bad novel, *Animal Farm*. The "rationale" underpinning this was that "people have more opportunity for sexual profligacy and indecency in city centre apartment blocks than in far-out, deracinated housing estates in which all public spaces are strictly controlled". And that's how McQuaid and O'Brien killed Herbert; with their obsession with sex.

Each detail of any proposed social housing scheme in Dublin had to go first and foremost for approval to McQuaid and O'Brien who at the time were great friends in faith. They regularly polished each other's rosary beads and drank each other's holy water. The archbishop wanted to control people living in these new areas so much so, that he had to personally rubber-stamp every architectural plan and design which at a time of frantic state house building meant Herbert was frazzled and worked to the edge of all physical and mental endurance fighting against and sadly encompassing some of their ever-changing diktats into his plans. Basically, the archbishop wanted to strictly limit any public spaces on which people might congregate to those that were under the direct auspices of his church. Anything else was communism and he would physically destroy any such ideologically poor plans presented to him with his very own bespoke length of rusty-nailed skirting board into your face like a hatchet.

'What do you mean a library? This is an outrage, a Trotskyist plot! What we need is another church, Mister Simms. One with a longer transept and a commensurate curving apse. Rendered in Portland stone methinks. Can't you see that, boy?'

Which meant, well built houses yes, but poorly socially-serviced that were very closely regulated and ruled by the church. To within an inch of people's lives according to Dr Rowley's theory as far as I can ascertain.

All this extra work and hassle by the church led Herbert to tragically commit suicide by jumping onto the railway tracks at Dun Laoghaire in 1948 and into the path of an on-coming train. The suicide note found on his person advised that overwork was threatening his sanity. He was the Corpo employee that worked himself to death. But perhaps he had a premonition that frescoed the church's future "plans and uses" for his Brutalist artworks in sinister sfumato. Or perhaps the archbishop told him out straight, he was a forthright man who always told it like it was, according to the history books. All that remains is for me to cherry this piece like all articles I've read about Herbert Simms, with the following quote. Warning: There will be tears.

"A tribute by Ernest F.N. Taylor, the city surveyor, was published in the *Irish Builder*: *'Behind a quiet and unassuming manner there lurked a forceful personality; and Mr Simms could uphold his point of view with a vigour that sometimes surprised those who did not know him well. By sheer hard work and conscientious devotion to duty, he has made a personal contribution towards the solution of Dublin's housing problem, probably unequalled by anyone in our time…It is not given to many of us to achieve so much in the space of a short lifetime for the benefit of our fellow men.'*"

Look out an upstairs window of any of Herbert's seventeen thousand legendary dwellings at end of day and you'll see an iridescent reinterpretation of Van Gogh's *Starry Night* twinkling before you. Then please do press play and listen to its music. Because in the city, there's seventeen thousand things he wants to say to you.

Other ways of Talking
by
Declan Geraghty

When we spoke
she polished less
a smidgen
a dab in between words
when there was silence the intensity of cleaning
gradually rose
if murky waters were encountered during conversation
she would clatter and rattle delph
when calm ground was found again and banter was
thrown in through moments of relief
the kettle would rise
along with humming that seemed more distant than it
was
the toaster would pop and we would mumble words in
between sups of tea and mouthfuls of toasts
and we'd talk quietly as we had run out of things to talk
about
and we'd make small talk in low voices
and she'd polish less
a dab in between words
the TV came on
a small one in the corner
it filled the room with pulsing light
coronation street was on
doesn't Ken Barlow look great for his age she said
he does I said
he does he said
there was silence

she polished less
then gradually more
I made my goodbyes
hugged them both
ahh you're not going are ye
sure ye only got here
ah I have to meet a friend I said
I made my way to the door
there was a silence behind me as I left
as I closed the door behind me it clinked
outside was dark
a car rattled passed
I waited a second before moving
then it was silent.

After Hours
by
Declan Geraghty

Pints Flowing
dropping like silk
craic going up and down in waves
calling you to throw in your intricate two cents
laser wit that could cut through steel
beaming beauty's bring you to foreign lands in a Dublin
backstreet boozer
results come through like Morse code telegram from
world war two
Fitzy's gone home and its getting sloppy now
angling prize nightmare memories
and the gargle is going down like reheated cabbage
water
dull thuds
thud
thud
ceiling wallpaper could have done with an extra coat
bells ring like bleak Christmas morning madness as
closing time approaches
cold drizzle traffic light haze upon me
sailing with the winds like a boat lost at sea
swerving back and forth but with some clear direction in
mind
taxi rank hoards march into battle positions
surly taxi driver fleeces me
back to the council estate with me
where reality will punish me in the morning.

Ireland is a Landlord
by
Declan Geraghty

It's just doors and walls
just a tiny spot of land
just plastic and wood
just tubes and metal
for water and heat
cables for light
a chair to sit down on between the walls
to rest your weary bones
walls to protect from the wind and cold
the roof from rain and elements
and it's all a trap,
it's all a set up
they have us on a hamsters wheel
just to have four walls
and a roof from the elements
and it gets heavier
the burden of rent
the pressure
until you can't afford to eat
or put on the heat
just breathe and wait
in the cold between four walls and a roof
not to mention the floor
although we get walked over as well
and there will come a time
when we all know when
when to stand up
and say no more no more to this madness.

(Published by Culture Matters UK April 2022)

A Drop Of Milk
by
John Finnan

It started with the face, as always. The weather last night had been savage, and the subtle yet sharp breeze had found several paths to his carefully covered torso. His face was pinched and red, the tip of nose felt as if it had been gnawed by cold teeth, and it was the pinching in his reddened cheeks which brought him around.

He couldn't do another night like this. Billy blinked in the early sun. He had survived another night. Despite his relative youth, the stiffness in his bones brought on by the harshness of his outdoor environment would have been more familiar in a man twice his age, racing towards arthritis.

He stretched, folded himself in a variety of positions and limbered up as best he could, totally unselfconsciously. He was long past caring what the average pedestrian would think of his morning routine, but here, tucked away in a seldom trafficked car park, there was no one to see. He relieved himself at a drain, shivering as the warm fluid left him, then grabbed his meagre belongings and entered the city.

Billy had all the usual trappings - cardboard sign, cup for donations, a tin whistle he played as best he could. And the other stuff, which life had not yet managed to take - hope, dignity, a functioning liver. Who knew how long they'd last?

Even the hope was turning - like milk left too long on the counter opposite the fridge. There were occasional traces of blood in his urine, so maybe he wouldn't have to worry about the dangers of alcoholism. He hoped so.

His morning walk was brisk, in an effort to bring some warmth to his muscles - he knew he'd be spending much of the day in a seated position of some sort. This was his effort to stay borderline active, despite the many times he didn't have any calories to spend on fruitless exercise.

Billy's meandering path had one destination - a corner shop that was still open, despite the CoVid plague that even Billy had heard about. He glanced at the headlines of the day, and took a second or two to find the weather forecast. Tonight would be worse.

He didn't want to have a confrontation with the guy in the shop, so a brief glance at the papers outside was all he permitted himself. And while he might on occasion resort to stealing food from some places, he never wanted to antagonise the staff here - it was a three minute refuge reading the headlines, turning one page, never hassling anyone and never being hassled. It didn't sound like much, but three minutes of normalcy was important. It helped him start the day.

Billy left the papers, and walked briskly on, away from the temptation of fruit which was lying unattended in boxes outside the shop. His stomach growled, but this was normal and while it never stopped being annoying, he'd learned how to ignore it. Temporarily at least.

As he walked, Billy started to think about what to do for later - the temperature was going to drop. He would do well to get indoors. There was always the Hostel option, but that was dependent on two key things - did they have space, and did he have the money. Right now, he had very little to his name. He had eaten yesterday morning, but yesterday had been another very quiet day in the city. Markedly fewer people were walking the streets these days, and it was not uncommon now for a day with the hand outstretched to remain empty for hours at a time.

Billy had a mental map of the area of the city he considered "his", and it was colour coded by the time of the day. Near the market for the morning, plenty of foot traffic even in these CoVid days, then he would take himself to the business centre about thirty minutes away. The white collar working stiffs were still going to their offices, though in reduced numbers. And though donations were typically fewer, what they lacked in frequency they made up for in size.

Afternoons were best spent in or near the park. You had more people in the park during the morning hours, but they were all jogging to beat the band, and they never stopped for anyone or anything. Afternoons were where people had lunch in the outdoors, and a full belly combined with a guilty conscience, in a satisfying monetary way.

Billy was set to be disappointed though. Today, for reasons best known to a godless and random chaotic universe, the market was mostly empty, the white collar workers ate at their desks, and the park gates were shuttered and closed to the public. There would be no help there, and no brief respite from the cold grey environs of the city.

As best he could, he alternated between standing and sitting near a fast-food restaurant. It was one of the few places still open that saw a pretty decent amount of traffic, because seated dining was forbidden. All their regular patrons were in and out of the doors within minutes. It kept him busy, but Billy's hands remained mostly empty.

There was some heat at least, coming out of the doors when they were opened. Even leaning back against the glass would provide relief, of a sort, from the chilly air. But he was unable to spend every minute next to their windows - it would have been bad for their business and the staff would have had no choice, he believed, but to see him off.

The downside of course, was that every time the door opened, there was the smell of freshly cooked warm food. It was maddeningly close, and a constant source of temptation. His willpower was sorely tested, as the twin needs of the body, warmth and hunger, waged a hormonally driven war for supremacy.

Once or twice, he chanced entering the premises to use the bathroom and drink from the taps. He did not dare try to perform anything close to a full wash, though he was meticulous about leaving the facilities clean and washing his hands (and yes, his face) as best he could in the mental time he allotted to himself. If the staff was aware of his presence, they said nothing, and for that he was grateful.

He went back outside, trying to avoid the eyes of the staff, certain that if he could see them up close, they'd have the usual mix of pity and revulsion with which he was becoming all too familiar. He'd rather turn his face towards a different kind of cold. At least for now.

It was approaching the hour of the Angelus when Billy, who was acutely aware of every penny in his pockets, finally had enough for a bed for the night. If he left now, he'd be certain, well pretty certain, of getting one of the available beds. He'd have a comfortable night in the warmth. But he doubted he'd be able to sleep - his stomach had been actively secreting all day, in a desperate state of constant readiness for food which had not arrived. His mouth was salivating at the thought.

From the shrinking bag of his intangible belongings, he took out a sliver of hope, and with it an idea wormed its way into his brain. He wanted to propose something. Setting his face as best he could remember to a look of honest sincerity, he opened the door and stepped inside.

Thomas was snapped out of his idle mental wanderings when the clearly homeless man approached his counter with obvious purpose. He had no mask. Thomas knew that this meant he was supposed to demand that the man leave. Corporate had decided they could refuse to serve any mask-less patron, and his supervisor (who he called "Karen" behind her back) said any violations of corporate policy would be written up. Thomas looked around. Karen was still AWOL, probably smoking out back, as usual. And on her phone, getting her jollies by swiping left over and over. To hell with her rules, and corporate.

He smiled this token defiance to himself, behind his own mask, and asked Billy what he could do for him.

"Hi," said Billy. "Look. I'd like to order some food. I have money," he emphasised this with one grubby five euro note and some coins in his hand, "but I was wondering if there was any chance I could maybe … work for the food? I know you're probably not hiring or anything, just some menial task, so I wouldn't have to spend what I got."

Thomas looked him up and down but didn't have an immediate answer.

"And look," said Billy, "if you can't, I understand. But is there any chance I could maybe eat it in here? It's warmer than outside. I'm not sick, and it's not like there's anyone else here."

Thomas looked him up and down again. "What the hell," he said, "will you clean the floors for me?" Next to cleaning the toilets, it was one job that Thomas despised more than any other. And having the staff do multiple jobs was one of the many cost-saving ideas Karen congratulated herself about.

"Yeah!" said Billy. "I'd be happy to!"

Thomas grinned, wider this time, and reached under the counter for a spare mask. "Here," he said. "Wear this. And if a blonde lady comes up to you and starts screaming, remember she's not your boss and there's no law against cleaning the floor."

A few minutes later, Thomas had directed Billy to the cleaning cart and was now taking his sweet time entering his order into the POS. His co-worker Carlos said to him "Karen's going to kill you Tommy."

"I'll clean it again if this guy fucks it up. It's one meal, and I'll put it through on employee discount. Give the guy a break."

"Your funeral man." Then they both attended to waiting customers.

Billy worked on the floor like an old pro. The queuing customers were socially distanced, giving him easy access to move between them, and while a few turned their noses up, most did not.

After a few minutes, Thomas called down to him. "Hey, buddy. Your meal's ready."

Billy glanced up at him, and his stomach growled again in eager anticipation. He suppressed it. "I'll finish paying for it first, if that's okay," he replied.

Thomas nodded, and went to the next customer. Billy returned to the job at hand, feeling productive for the first time in quite a while. After his meal, he'd go to the Hostel feeling warmer and well fed… and he'd have enough for a bed.

It didn't take him long. And soon, he was sitting quietly at a table to himself, eating heartily and feeling just fine.

"What the fuck is this, Thomas?" The shrill angry sound echoed across the many metalled surfaces of the kitchen area. Thomas groaned quietly. "What?"

A small overweight manageress marched over to the young man, with one angry finger outstretched accusingly. "What's this I hear about you giving free food to the homeless?" she shrieked.

"I didn't give him anything for free. He ordered it. I served him. He has a mask and everything," protested Thomas.

"Only because you gave him one bro," called a voice from some eavesdropping co-worker in the kitchen.

"I can check the video you know!" berated the angry woman. "I better see him handing money over to you. And god help you if your till is short tonight!"

The little blonde dervish spun, signalling the confrontation was over, but Thomas was having none of it.

"He's homeless, but he's still a person. Can you just act like a person for once and let him eat his meal in peace?"

She whip-lashed back to get in Thomas's face and practically screamed at him. "That's it! You're fired!"

Thomas glanced briefly at the waiting customer who had the misfortune to be next in line. "Sorry ma'am. I'm sure this "Karen" here will order someone to help you shortly. She can't make any food herself. It's too much like actual work."

He studiously ignored the ensuing freak out, and wandered over to where Billy was quietly eating his food.

"Everything good?" asked Thomas.
"Yeah, it's great," said Billy. "Look do you want me to talk to her, see if I can tell her it wasn't your fault?"

Billy briefly thought about offering the cash he had, to become a regular paying customer, but couldn't bring himself to do it.

"Don't worry about it," said Thomas. "I was going to get fired for something. Might as well have been for acting like a decent human being."

The manager's screams and angry rantings had finally brought security to the table. Billy recognised the type easily. He'd been moved on from various premises often enough. So it was to his great surprise that the guard gestured for him to stay seated.

"I saw what you did Thomas," said the security guard. "And I saw you, sir. I liked that you finished the floor before you took your seat."

He eyed the seated man up and down, as if mentally assessing him. "My security firm is hiring," he said. "Lots of the stores that are still open right now, need someone to act as doorman. It's boring work, but it pays. You'd count people coming in and out, maybe face a few angry types who don't think the rules should apply to them." His head tilted to the side, and said "It may not last long, but we need people now. Interested?"

It started with the face, as it often did. Warm tears from above, and a blooming heat from his mask covered cheeks.

Thomas wished him good luck and then he and Billy touched elbows, in that curious nu-greeting which had been adopted by people too fearful to be close, yet still reachable by slow moving ripples across a sea of human kindness.

Freedom at Last
by
Nicholas Earley

I hadn't even noticed a sign post when I took a left turn. I'd just wanted to get off the main road, pull in somewhere, anywhere, just so long as I didn't have to keep looking at the same road. Mile after continuous mile. I'd just jumped into the car to get away from the house. That house, that granite house I called home. They say home is where the heart is, well there is no heart there now since she'd left. Not a word spoken between us, no hint of a warning that she was going. The only sign she'd left was her paw marks on the floor where she'd made her way through the escape hatch in the porch door. That's the thanks I'd gotten after taking her in off the streets.

Bitch.

Of Course I didn't know it was goodbye, I just took it for granted she'd stay with me forever.

How wrong could I be. She was just like the women in my life. They only stayed with me till they got what they wanted, so why should Samantha be any different. To hell with them all. I finally came to my senses when my neighbour came over to tell me that Jake was missing too. He'd disappeared the same time as Samantha. My neighbour took it real bad, said he'd had Jake since he was a pup. He took to the booze then, began to beat his wife with the dog leash. She's now separated from him, he's only allowed visit the kids once a year. I send him a card anonymously on St Valentine's Day, just to let him think somebody still wants him.

It was when he told me about Jake going missing, that I started remembering all the little things about them that I'd shoved in the back of my mind, too innocent to see what was staring me in the face. Like the time I found them both naked in Samantha's Kennel. Jake standing up on his hind legs to kiss my hand, pretending there was nothing going on. Then Jake no longer wrapped his paws around my leg to hump it, now I know why, he was too busy doing the real thing. Then there was her speckled coloured rubber ball, the one she always insisted on bringing with us to the park.

I'd blame Jake on robbing it when I found it in his garden. Looking back now it was probably her who'd given it to him. Then there was her other odds and ends I'd found in his garden. Now I realise how foolish I must have looked ringing up the police anonymously to report Jake for being a cat burglar.

The stupid dog, he'd probably fallen for her the way I had when I'd first seen her standing at the rubbish bin, her cute nose covered with dirt. The rain that had just recently fallen was still dripping from her coat as she looked at me with those deep brown eyes. It was a cinch to fall for the stare. She didn't hesitate for a second when I flicked my fingers. She just jumped straight into my arms, ruining my suit with her muddy paws. But I didn't care, it was that look she gave me, it just oozed appeal, right down to the end of her tail.

After bringing her home, I vowed that she'd want for nothing. As a bachelor, it was easy for her to take over my heart. I had just split up recently after a fifteen month relationship with a pygmy I'd met through a dating agency. I have subsequently found out that the dating agency was really a front for transvestite rugby players. My so called partner for life had walked out on me just a week before I found Samantha. She claimed I'd been picking arguments with her over the least thing, she also accused me of leaving food out of her reach. She said the final straw was when I insisted on leaving the remote control on top of the television.

In a way I wasn't sorry she'd gone. I'd gotten tired of listening to the noise of her platform shoes as she traipsed up and down the stairs. I'd even had a lower door inserted in the main door for easy access for her. But for all her faults and she had four hundred and eighty seven of them, I still missed her. Of course even when she was here I still missed her, but that's neither here nor there. By the way if you should happen to meet a blond three foot three pygmy with blonde eyebrows, a blonde moustache and a hump on her back, who answers to the nick name Sancha Siminov Betiga Arivee, tell her Pete was asking for her.

She was just like all the other women in my life, ungrateful. There was Olga with the club foot. She'd managed to escape through the Berlin wall battering a hole in it with her head.

Two months she'd lived with me. Although she couldn't speak a word of English, she had the uncanny knack of always managing to complete the crossword in the Sunday Times. During our cultural exchanges she showed me how to squeeze out blackheads and build a bomb shelter. We managed to conduct our love life without any sex, which I found to be quite exhilarating.

She always went to bed with a picture of Stalin inside her bra. It was on her birthday when I bought her a hand glider that she flew out of my life for good.

Then before Olga there was Consuela, a knife thrower from Brazil. I had met her in a pub in town, for whom she played on the darts team. She was on the run from the British secret service for having in her possession substantial proof as regards to Margaret Thatcher's state of mind when she was leader of the conservative government. The evidence clearly showed that Mrs Thatcher had been brain dead for the past twenty years. I had to hide her up in the attic and it was there I allowed her practice her knife throwing. This she managed to do by tying me to a tractor wheel which was fitted to an axel on the wall. All the cuts and nicks she'd inflicted on my body as I spun round the room at thirty seven miles an hour seemed less painful compared to the sight of seeing her walk out of my life with a one armed guitar player called lefty Gonzalez.

When Consuela left I got a severe pain in the heart. I later felt foolish when the doctor pointed out this was due to a staple imbedded in my shirt. I contemplated suicide and went as far as employing a professional killer to do the job. What I didn't know was that he was illiterate and couldn't read my name properly. To this present day he is still going around shooting anyone with the name Pete. I have since found out I could have done the job cheaper by buying one of the faulty cookers that the gas company has for sale. However there is probably no need for any of these methods as in the meantime I have since become employed and with the new government in place there is a good possibility I'll starve to death. Failing all of this, there is one option left to me. There is one last place of sanctuary in which I can find some peace of mind. Where once and for all, women and the temptation of the flesh can be curbed. I could become a parish priest.

About the Authors

Liz Smith

Liz Smith is an artist and works as a Creative Social Inclusion Officer at ReCreate. Originally from Inchicore, Liz has a Degree in Fine Art Sculpture and an MA in Socially Engaged Art from NCAD. In 2001, Liz began facilitating children's art workshops and since 2015, has expanded her practice to facilitating collaborative community projects that tackle social and personal issues. Liz has a strong drawing practice using portraiture to reframe her disability and question social injustices. She is honored to have been invited to contribute to this publication.

Rob Doyle

Rob Doyle was born in Dublin. His first novel, Here Are the Young Men, was chosen as a book of the year by the Sunday Times, Irish Times and Independent, and was among Hot Press magazine's '20 Greatest Irish Novels 1916-2016'. Doyle has adapted it for film with director Eoin Macken. Other works by Rob Doyle include This Is The Ritual, Threshold and Autobibliography.

John Healy

John Healy is the author of the novels *The Grass Arena*, *The Streets Above Us*, *Coffee House Chess Tactics* and *The Metal Mountain*. His novel *The Grass Arena* was made into a movie starring Mark Rylance. He's won the Pen Ackerley award, Europe's top prize for literary autobiography. The first book in the history of the prize to win the award outright. The book and the film of the book have gained between them over a dozen major national and international awards.

Frankie Gaffney

Frankie Gaffney is a writer from Dublin. His bestselling debut novel, Dublin Seven, described by the Irish Times as "Love/Hate meets Ulysses" was published to critical acclaim and controversy in 2015.

Kit de Waal

Kit de Waal was born in Birmingham to an Irish mother, who was a childminder and foster carer and a Caribbean father. She worked for fifteen years in criminal and family law, was a magistrate for several years and sits on adoption panels. She used to advise Social Services on the care of foster children, and has written training manuals on adoption, foster care and judgecraft for members of the judiciary. Author of the The Trick to Time, My Name is Leon, Supporting Cast, Becoming Dinah and Six Foot Six.

Elizabeth Reapy

Elizabeth Reapy is a writer from Co. Mayo. She is the author of novels Red Dirt and Skin, and has an MA in Creative Writing from Queen's University in Belfast. Her debut novel Red Dirt won the best Newcomer of the year Award in 2016 and the 2017 Irish Rooney Prize.

Kevin Higgins

Kevin Higgins has been described by The Stinging Fly magazine as "likely the most read living poet in Ireland. His sixth full collection of poems 'Ecstatic' will be published by Salmon in June 2021.

Dave Lordan

Dave Lordan is the author of the poetry collections *THE BOY IN THE RING* (2007), which won the Patrick Kavanagh Award, the Shine/Strong Award, and was shortlisted for the *IRISH TIMES* poetry award, and *INVITATION TO A SACRIFICE* (2010). His play *JO BANGLES* was produced by the Eigse Riada company in 2010. In 2011 Lordan received the Ireland Chair of Poetry Bursary. He is an editor at *THE BOGMAN'S CANNON* and contributors to Arena, the arts program for RTE.

Paula Meehan

Irish poet and playwright Paula Meehan was born in working-class Dublin and earned degrees from Trinity College and Eastern Washington University. She is the author of the poetry collections *Return and No Blame* (1984); *Reading the Sky* (1986); *The Man Who Was Marked by Winter* (1991; US edition 1994); *Pillow Talk* (1994); *Mysteries of the Home* (1996); *Dharmakaya* (2001), which won a Denis Devlin Award; *Six Sycamores* (2004), with the artist Marie Foley; and *Painting Rain* (2009). Her plays for children and adults have been staged widely and performed for radio. Meehan has also held workshops with inner-city communities and in prisons. Her numerous honours and awards include the Marten Toonder Award, the Butler Literary Award, and the post of Ireland Professor of Poetry. In 2015, she was inducted into the Hennessy Hall of Fame for her achievements in poetry.

Gerard Lee

Gerard Lee is an actor and writer. His novel Forsaken is published by New Island Books, and his plays have been presented in theatres around Dublin, including M*angan's Last Gasp* (on James Clarence Mangan) and *A New Day*, both produced by Bewley's Café Theatre, *This Old Man* at the Viking, *One Is Not Oneself* (based on a selection of Noel Coward songs) at the New Theatre, and *Unlucky for Some* (two monologues) at Theatre Upstairs.

Chris Agee

Chris Agee is a poet, essayist, photographer and editor. He was born in San Francisco on a US Navy hospital ship and grew up in Massachusetts, New York and Rhode Island. After high school at Phillips Academy Andover and a year in Aix-en-Provence, France, he attended Harvard University and since graduation has lived in Ireland. His third collection of poems, *Next to Nothing* (Salt, 2008), was shortlisted in Britain for the 2009 Ted Hughes Award for New Work in Poetry, and its sequel, *Blue Sandbar Moon* (The Irish Pages Press), appeared in 2018. He is the Editor of *Irish Pages*, and edited *Balkan Essays* (The Irish Pages Press, 2016), the sixth volume of Hubert Butler's essays, published simultaneously in Croatian by the Zagreb publishing house Fraktura. His new poetic work, *Trump Rant* (The Irish Pages Press, 2021), has just been published. He lives in Belfast, and divides his time between Ireland, Scotland and Croatia.

Fran Lock

Fran Lock is a some-time itinerant dog-whisperer, the author of numerous chapbooks and seven poetry collections, most recently *Contains Mild Peril* (Out-Spoken Press, 2019) and *Ruses and Fuses* (Culture Matters, 2019), the last in a trilogy of works with collage artist Steev Burgess. Fran has two projects forthcoming this year from Pamenar Press and Poetry Bus Press respectively. She is an associate editor at Culture Matters, and edits the Soul Food column for *Communist Review*.

Alan Morrison

Alan Morrison's poetry collections include *A Tapestry of Absent Sitters* (Waterloo, 2009), *Keir Hardie Street* (Smokestack Books, 2010), *Captive Dragons* (Waterloo, 2011), *Blaze a Vanishing/ The Tall Skies* (Waterloo, 2013), *Shadows Waltz Haltingly* (Lapwing, 2015), *Tan Raptures* (Smokestack, 2017), *Shabbigentile* (Culture Matters, 2019), *Gum Arabic* (Cyberwit, 2020), and *Anxious Corporals* (Smokestack, 2021). Poems and monographs have appeared in such journals as *The International Times, The Journal, The London Magazine, The Morning Star, Poetry Monthly, Poetry Salzburg, Red Poets,* and *Stand.* He was joint winner of the Bread & Roses Poetry Prize 2018. His poetry has been awarded grants from Arts Council England, the Royal Literary Fund, the Society of Authors and the Oppenheim-John Downes Memorial Trust. He edits international webzine *The Recusant* (www.therecusant.org.uk). Website: www.alanmorrison.co.uk

Liz Gillis

Historian and author Liz Gillis is from the Liberties. She has a Degree in Irish History and currently works as a Researcher for the History Show on RTE Radio. She is the author of six books about the Irish Revolution including, 'Women of the Irish Revolution' and 'The Hales Brothers and the Irish Revolution' and is co-organiser of the annual conference on the Burning of the Custom House in 1921. In 2018 Liz was a recipient of the Lord Mayor's Award for her contribution to history.

Karl Parkinson

Karl Parkinson is a writer from inner-city Dublin. *The Blocks* his début novel was published to critical acclaim in 2016 by New Binary Press. In 2013 Wurmpress published his début poetry collection, *Litany of the City and Other Poems*, his second poetry collection, *Butterflies of a Bad Summer*, was published by Salmon in 2016, and his third collection of poetry *Sacred Symphony*, was published in 2020 by Culture Matters. His work has appeared in many anthologies, *New Planet Cabaret* (New Island Press) and *If Ever You Go: A Map of Dublin in Poetry and Song* (Dedalus Press), *The Deep Hearts core: Irish poets revisit a touchstone poem* (Dedalus Press), *Children of the nation* and *From the plough to the stars*(Culture matters). His work has been published in *The Irish Times* and *RTE Culture, The Dublin Inquirer,* and *The Stinging Fly.*

Anne Tannam

Anne Tannam is the author of two poetry collections with a third 'Twenty-six Letters of a New Alphabet' forthcoming from Salmon Poetry later this year. For more information on Anne's poetry, visit her website at www.annetannampoetry.ie

Cheryl Vail

Cheryl Vail, originally from New Jersey now calling Dublin home, has been writing since she could scribble on any available surface. Her poems can be found in Issue V of *Sonder* Magazine, on *Culture Matters* website, and in issue three of *The Waxed Lemon*.

Viviana Fiorentino

Viviana Fiorentino is Italian and lives in Belfast where she teaches Italian. An award-winning poet in Italy, her poems, short stories and translations have appeared in international literature magazines (as Nazione Indiana, FourXFour NI, Poethead, The Blue Nib, Paris Lit Up, Honest Ulsterman, Mantis - journal of the Stanford University, The Trumpet 9, Abridged). In 2019, her poems appeared in the anthology '*Writing Home*' (Dedalus Press); in 2021, in the anthology '*Days of Clear Light - A Festschrift in Honour of Jessie Lendennie & in Celebration of Salmon Poetry at 40*' (Salmon Poetry). In Italy, she published a poetry collection (Controluna Press), in anthology (Arcipelago Itaca Edizioni) and a novel (Transeuropa Publishing House). She co-founded two activist poetry initiatives (Sky, You Are Too Big and Letters With Wings) and Le Ortique (forgotten women artists blog).

Glenn Gannon
Glenn Gannon is a writer and actor from the Liberties Dublin. He is the author of the book *Miracle Man : From Homeless To Hollywood*. He is an advocate for the homeless and an ambassador for the Dublin Simon Community. He has appeared in numerous films including *Laws of Attraction*, *Turning Green*, *The oOld Curiosity Shop* and *Becoming Jane*.

Eimear Grace
Eimear Grace lives in Dublin and is a member of Ballyfermot Writers' Group. She writes poems, plays, flash fiction and novels. She loves the simple act of putting pen to paper and using words to create something new and original. She believes the process of writing is in itself its own reward.

Dylan Henvey
Dylan Henvey is a playwrite and short story writer from Ballyfermot. His play "*Once upon a time in west Dublin*" featured in the "Dublin festival of history 2019".

He had a rehearsed reading of his piece "*Animals*" in Smock Alley as part of the "Scene and Heard festival" in February 2020. It was the first rehearsed reading to have sold out in the history of the "Scene and Heard festival". (Mainly due to Dylan buying up tickets on his credit card and then forcing them on everyone and anyone he's ever met.)

Orla Fay

Orla Fay, from County Meath edits *Drawn to the Light Press*, a new online magazine of poetry. Her chapbook *Drawn to the Light* was published in October 2020, and her first full collection is forthcoming from Salmon Poetry. She edited *Boyne Berries* for six years. Her work has appeared in *Poetry Ireland Review*, *Cyphers*, *The Irish Times*, *The SHOp*, *Abridged*, *The Stony Thursday Book, The Ogham Stone*, *Skylight 47*, *Crannóg, The Honest Ulsterman*, and *The Ireland Chair of Poetry Commemorative Anthology*. She won 3rd prize in The Jonathan Swift Creative Writing Awards 2020 and was also commended in The Francis Ledwidge Poetry Award 2020. She blogs at https://orlafay.blogspot.com/. Twitter@FayOrla.

Patricia Kane

Patricia came to writing late in life. She is a member of The Ballyfermot writers group and has had a number of pieces published through the group.

Helen Sullivan

Helen joined the Ballyfermot Writers Group in September 2017 she had a short story. The Cottage That Wasn't a Cottage, published in The Flying Superhero Clothes Horse. The following year she had a poem, The Streets with No Pity and a short story, St Michan's Mummy published in Mustang Bally. Helen has also written a book Darkwood Forest, a fantasy novel for YA and hopes to have it published one day.

Natasha Helen Crudden

Natasha Helen Crudden is a punk-influenced performance poet, musician and author of poetry collections "Barbed-Wire Cage" and "Ctrl/Alt/Delete" and novel "Empire Evolution". Her work has been published in several literary publications and her performance resume includes the Electric Picnic festival and main stage in Whelan's, Dublin. She is a regular on the Dublin open mic scene and performs at arts nights throughout Ireland.

Alan O'Brien

Bricklayer by trade, raised in the Finglas/Ballymun area of Dublin. In opposition to *emigration culture*, returned to education in 2011 receiving a BA in English and History and an Oral History Certificate and then subsequently gave himself permission to write a bit more. Shortlisted for the Maeve Binchy Travel Award 2015; winner of the P.J. O'Connor Award (shhhhhhhh) 2016, Co-wrote, directed and took a part in a play relating to the 1916 Rising, performed exactly 100 years from the seminal Irish event in the cradle of the revolution itself, Liberty Hall. He continues to write while also working as a skilled tradesman.

Paul Lee

Paul Lee has worked as an actor on stage and TV and has been a promoter (www.musiclee.ie) and venue manager on the Dublin music scene for over thirty years.

Andrea Lovric

Andrea Lovric is a Croatian writer who's lived in in Dublin since 2015. She has work published in her native language in "*Rec u mrezi*" and "*Cro Zimske Price*". She is also a regular contributor of short pieces to magazines.

Nancy Dawn (Nancy Matchton Owens)

Nancy was born in long Island, NY. She graduated with a Bachelor of fine arts in Theatre and a minor in Psychology from Emerson college, in Boston, USA. She is an actress and writer who writes poetry and short stories and co-wrote and performed in an original play in The Axis Theatre called "*How safe are your secrets*"? Most recently she has incorporated well- being and mindfulness for Trinity nursing student department and hopes for this part of the creativity to expand. In the last five years she has facilitated the Ballymun Writers group for Dublin city council. Nancy is also part of a Musical Duo that has performed throughout Europe and North America

Faith Malone

Faith Malone is a short story writer and poet from Clondalkin. She has previously published work in "*What's The Stories?*", a short story collection which was released by Roddy Doyle and "*Fighting Words*" in 2017. She is currently studying Fashion Buying and Merchandising.

Victoria Gilbert

Victoria Gilbert is a poet and writer from Inchicore. She is currently working on her first poetry collection. Her poem splitting seeds is dedicated to her sister Lynn who passed away last year.

Robert Smyth

A child of the 70's. Grew up in North Dublin. Writing since an early age. I used to be an avid reader. Nowadays I dip in and out when I get the chance. I reflect on what I see around me when I'm writing. I love to put pen to paper. I share my life with my beautiful Wife. She supports my writing and encourages me greatly. I still live in North Dublin but a different place to where I grew up. I work part time to support myself.

Órla Gately

Órla Gately is a student from Dublin, currently studying at Trinity College. Her poem considers the pandemic which has taken a toll on all, none more so than the homeless. Órla is passionate about poetry. The poem 'Room 412' by Órla appeared in '*Teaching English*' magazine as a junior prize winner.

Claire Galligan

Claire Galligan founded theatre in prisons in Ireland in the 1980's. Her theatre company 'Exit' won three awards in the first P.J. O'Connor competition in R.T.E.Claire subsequently won the Harvey's of Bristol Award for her contribution to the Arts. She trained as a director at the National Theatre London and Circle Rep. New York. She has directed nationally and internationally in the U.S.A., Vatican Rome, and represented Ireland at the Theatre Festival Egypt. Claire has written and produced three plays for Radio and a documentary 'Out of the Dark.' She has just completed her Memoir.

Richard O'Shea

Norsam aka Richard O'Shea is a Mayo man who has lived in Dublin over the past 20 years. He's a Poet, word speaker and general ranter. A regular on the spoken word scene, he writes about personal and current subjects that some people don't always get into. He believes strongly in free speech and that nothing should be censored and that every opinion deserves to be at least heard.

Joanne Cullivan

Joanne Cullivan lives in Dublin. She has been writing for the last few years. She enjoys writing short stories across all genres, mostly comedy. She is part of the Inkslingers Writing Group based in the Irish Writers Centre. Some of her stories have been published in their anthologies.

R.G. Bighiu

R.G. Bighiu is a polifacetic author rhyming her way through Romania, France and Spain just to arrive in Ireland where in her time off she helps some graffiti artists and meets the local and not so local wizards and witches. She tries to put it all together in the only permanent home she gets, which is online at: https://rgbcreates.com/.

Violeta Geraghty

Violeta Geraghty is a young Irish Spanish poet from Madrid. When she's not writing her hobbies include gymnastics and swimming.

Catriona Murphy

Catriona Murphy won an award for a short story in 2008, from the SCC Creative Writing competition, and hasn't stopped writing since. She lives in Dublin, Ireland and works full-time in digital marketing.

Sinéad MacDevitt

Sinéad MacDevitt has been published in *Boyne Berries, Extended Wings, Revival Literary Journal, Heart of Kerry, North West Words, The Reform Jewish Quarterly, The Flying Superhero Clothes Horse, Mustang Bally* and *2020 Visions*. She was short-listed for the *Swords Heritage Festival* short story competition and highly commended for the *Jonathan Swift* prose competition. Her poems have been commended for the *Francis Ledwidge*, *LMFM* poetry and *Rush* Poetry competition. She was awarded second place for the *Desmond O'Grady* poetry competition. She was also a winner of the *Little Gems* poetry competition.

Brendan Canning

Brendan Canning is a writer from Ballyfermot. He writes haiku, poetry and short stories in English and Irish.

Derek Copley

Derek Copley is a traditional musical from, and living in, Ballyfermot. An occasional writer of songs and fiction (and fictional songs), he also runs the Ballyer Trad Hub, which helps prompt the playing – and heritage – of traditional music within Ballyfermot.

Erinna Behal
Erinna Behal is an artist and writer based in Dublin 8 and a member of the Ballyfermot Writer's Group. A native of Killarney, Co. Kerry, she draws on personal experiences of homelessness, housing insecurity and the interconnected social complications of an undiagnosed autism spectrum disorder.

Joseph Plowman
Joseph Plowman is a clinical and cognitive behavioural hypnotherapist born in Dublin. He has degrees in psychology and applied psychology, and writes and tutors in psychology, child psychology and mental health awareness. Clinically, with hypnosis and through talk therapy, he sees time and again the power of words to change experience, to alter thinking and feeling, and to beget new behaviour. As Freud noted, words were originally magic. Words can also advocate for those who have no voice. Or home. It is our thinking, our feeling, and our behaviour as a society, which needs to change.
Website: www.phenomenalpsychology.com

Joseph Anthony O'Connor
Joseph Anthony O'Connor, from Ballyfermot, Dublin, is a songwriter, poet, singer, scriptwriter. His musical play FLYNN, a homage to the late, great Irish poet Patrick Kavanagh, premiered at the Abbey Theatre in November 2017 to honour the 50th anniversary of the poet's death. His three poems featured in this book, 'Waiting For The Curer'; 'My Time In England' & 'Thieves In The Temple Bar' are examples from each of the three distinct categories in the volume of poems which he is currently seeking to have published.

Camillus John

Camillus John was born and braised in Dublin. He has had work published in *The Stinging Fly*, *RTÉ Ten*, *The Lonely Crowd* and other such organs. He would also like to mention that Pats won the FAI cup in 2014 after 52 miserable years of not winning it.

Declan Geraghty

Declan Geraghty is a writer and poet from Dublin. He's had short stories published in various collections most notably *"From the Plough to the Stars"* published by Culture Matters UK, and *"Dublin in the Coming Times"* which was edited by Roddy Doyle. He's had poetry published in *"Cry of the Poor"* and *"The Brown Envelope book"*. His latest publication is a short story in the collection *"Knock and Enter"* edited by Declan Burke. He's had work published in online magazines *Epoque Press*, *Gnashing teeth publications* and *Blognostics*. He's currently studying Creative Writing and Cultural Studies.

John Finnan

John writes mostly with the Ballymun Writers group. His poetry and short stories have been appearing in various anthologies since 2007.

Nicholas Earley

Nicholas Earley was a writer and poet from Dublin. He's had short stories and poetry featured in Ballyer press publications *"The flying superhero clothes horse"*, *"Mustang Bally"* and *"Visions 2020"*.

About Ballyfermot Writers' Group

Supported and facilitated by Ballyfermot library and Dublin City Council's Public Libraries Division, Ballyfermot Writers' Group was established in 2016. They meet with a ping every second Wednesday in Ballyfermot library from 6.30 p.m.

In May 2017, they were chosen to host an event, Between the Bookcases, which was part of the International Literature Festival Dublin 2017 comprising songs, stories, sketches and conceptual art. The comedian and writer, Kevin Gildea, worked with the group on this event.

In 2018, they were again chosen to host an event in the International Literature Festival Dublin to launch their first anthology celebrating Ballyfermot's 70th birthday entitled The Flying Superhero Clothes Horse 2018 – Ballyer is 70! This event was launched by Broadcaster Joe Duffy, singer-songwriter, Declan O'Rourke and playwright, Jimmy Murphy, who also made contributions to the anthology along with Neville Thompson, Finbar Furey, Kevin Gildea and Ken Larkin.

In 2019, Declan Geraghty from the Ballyfermot group, and John Finnan from the Ballymun group collaborated and produced an anthology entitled Mustang Bally, with contributions by many members of the two writing groups. It was launched like a rocket in Pearse Street library in May 2019.

In 2020, Declan Geraghty and John Finnan, went solo once again and produced a book of poetry entitled Visions 20-20 containing contributions from many members of the Ballyfermot and Ballymun groups as well as further afield. Covid-19 prevented an official launch but it probably would have broken the internet into smithereens.

New members are always welcome. Simply contact Ballyfermot library for more information.

How it works

Unholster your pencil and write creatively on the spot to a bespoke, tinselled prompt given out on the night. Then read what you've written to the group for lavish praise, iridescent bouquets and international awards. Or bring prepared writing along with you and read that if you wish. The choice is yours.

Just turn up on the night with your own pencil

Thanks to all the writers who contributed to this collection. Special thanks to Artist Liz Smith for the cover art. Thanks to John Healy, writer of The Grass Arena and Glenn Gannon Writer of Miracle Man for contributing. Both writers autobiographies give glimpses into the hardships of homelessness.

All profits from this book go to The Dublin Simon Community.

Ballyer Press

Also By Ballyer Press

The Flying Superhero Clothes Horse 2018

Ballyer is 70!

Ballyfermot is a community bustling with creativity since its inauguration by magic wand and monster puff of smoke back in 1948. That's exactly seventy years ago in 2018. To mark this glorious occasion, Ballyfermot Writers' Group, with very special guests, has published this bespoke selection of songs, stories, art and flying superhero clothes horses with all profits being donated to The Simon Community. Come and have a read if you think you're bionic enough!

Featuring Finbar Furey, Neville Thompson, Declan O'Rourke, Joe Duffy, Jimmy Murphy, Kevin Gildea, Ken Larkin, Portraits n Stuff and the members of Ballyfermot Writers' Group.

And by The Ballymun Writers and featuring the writers from Ballyfermot

Mustang Bally (2019)

An anthology of poetry and prose,

available from Amazon.

Edited and compiled by Declan Geraghty, John Finnan and Camillus John. Cover Art by Liz Smith.

Thanks to Dublin City Council and Ballyfermot Library for supporting Ballyfermot Creative Writers Group.

Ballyer Press

Dedicated to Nicholas Earley

This book is dedicated to Nicholas Earley or as he was known to us "Nicky". He died on the 13th of October 2020 and was a member of the Ballyfermot writers group.

As I write this note as a tribute to Nicky we are still in lockdown in Ireland. Every day the news gets a little better with vaccines coming through, so maybe this is the last phase of it until some type of normality returns. Myself, Rodney and Helen attended Nicky's funeral but unfortunately we couldn't get into the church, because of Covid restrictions only allowing for close family.

We waited in the court yard of the church and gave our condolences to his wife and daughter Audrey. We waited in the court yard in the drizzle and cold and listened to the ceremony playing through a loud speaker outside. After about forty five minutes I made my way home.

My farewell to my old friend went past with a whimper. With the pandemic still raging, I couldn't really process the death of Nicky as there was just to much anxiety and uncertainty everywhere. It will hit me later for sure, and when our writing group opens up again and we are all in person. That is when it will probably sting the most.

Nicky was a self-educated working class man from inner city Dublin who eventually settled in Ballyfermot. He was a great comedy writer and poet, and gave us all a great laugh at our writers group meetings. He had a great sense of humour and it came through hilarious and peculiar in his writings. Some of his most impressive pieces were on more serious political and social issues though. I think this showed how much of an all-round writer he was.

I would like to thank his daughter Audrey for allowing us to publish some of his work in this collection. Hopefully this book can be a proper farewell to him from all his friends in the Ballyfermot writers group who'll miss him very much. We will miss the craic we had and Nicky will not be forgotten for sure.

Rest in Peace Nicky

Declan Geraghty

Printed in Great Britain
by Amazon